MOTHER KNOWS BEST

WITH AN INTRODUCTION BY SADIE HARTMANN

GWENDOLYN KISTE   KRISTI DEMEESTER

KELSEA YU   RACHEL HARRISON

AND MANY MORE

EDITED BY

LINDY RYAN

EDITOR OF *INTO THE FOREST*

Dedication
To our mothers and their daughters.

TABLE OF CONTENTS

PREFACE
by Lindy Ryan

In INTO THE FOREST, Baba Yaga—the most ambiguous and villainous woman of fairy-tale lore—provided a ready muse for tales of wildness and wickedness. Indeed, this fearsome, forest-dwelling, child-eating witch is more than the sum of her stories. A goddess, a hag, a bender and breaker of convention and expectations, she is a cautionary tale for and about powerful women.

She is Grandmother Witch to us all.

Perhaps most important today, Baba Yaga is "womanhood personified, power and paradox, equal parts feared and beloved[1]." She represents duality incarnate: a sympathetic heart and an iron-toothed hunger. She is meant to be feared—in particular by children and particularly by young girls. She is Maiden and Crone, but most of all, she is Mother.

And there's something, of course, to be said about girls and their mothers.

Like Baba Yaga, mothers wield tremendous power—power that can calm or cut, harm or heal, nurture or needle. A mother provides and polices her children, alternately stitching

---

[1]   Ryan, L. (2023). "The Unapology of Baba Yaga." In J. Provine & J. Sullivan (Eds.), *A Compendium of Creeps: World folklore, haunted locales, and original fiction.* Cemetery Gates Media.

us together and slicing open our seams. Sometimes, she is the savior, tucking us into our warm bed at night. Other times, she is the monster waiting under it.

Motherhood itself is a monstrous process. The slow, bloody affair of creation, visceral and violent in its impulses, ferocious in its affections. So much is a mother's heart capable of. So unconditional her love. So sublime her gaze.

So enduring her influence.

Mothers are made, not born. They become, and they beget daughters who, sometimes, become mothers. Sometimes, they become just like their mothers.

And the last thing any girl wants to be is just like her mother.

This anthology is for all the mothers and all the mothered.

FOREWORD

by Sadie Hartmann, "Mother Horror"

A word about mothers.

Not all mothers, of course. Just some.

An eternal mother worshipped for a thousand generations. A once-in-a-lifetime kind of mother. That kind of mother doesn't happen by accident.

She is created into being through careful intention.

It is essential for special mothers to feel good about themselves, no matter the cost.

Any coping mechanism will do.

Gaslighting.

Blaming and shaming.

Excuses.

Denial.

Projecting.

Smothering.

Mothers have a dark, pitch-black void inside them. A wound. The wound is a flaw that must be covered up. There is a core belief that flaws are a weakness that leads to worthlessness. Mothers must be special, perfect–a treasure!

Other mothers embrace their imperfections.

Mediocrity.

Normalcy.

These are not *real* mothers.

To be celebrated and memorialized, there are particular behaviors and specific disciplines.

Methods.

You must rewrite history.

If anything paints the mother in a bad light...

Suggests otherwise...

The narrative must be recognized, minimized, and then trivialized.

Children will complain.

They will insist there are monsters under the bed that eat everyone they love except you.

It isn't true.

They're lying.

Daughters will refuse to follow in your footsteps, follow your lead, and listen to reason.

Convince them.

Manipulate. Control.

Children are curious. They're always poking around where they don't belong. They ask silly questions. They look for secrets and get into trouble.

Punish. Lock them away.

Children grow up. They get older and wiser, less dependent on their mothers. There are ways to make sure they never leave you.

Start early! You must sow seeds of doubt as soon as you can. Maturity creeps up like an invasive weed in a garden: wrapping hearty tendrils around a young child's heart, supplying extra strength.

Snip! Cut!

Quickly tie those apron strings! Extra tight, just in case.

Suffocate. Eradicate.

Whip up a batch of Mother's medicine... Not to get better, no... To get worse.

You are the voice of reason. You are the last word.

Silence the other voices. The other influences.

You are the only thing a child needs. Help them lean not on their own understanding of the world they live in or the feelings they have but on your interpretation.

No right.

No wrong.

Just Mother's advice. Mother knows best.

The love and adoration of your family is the air you breathe.

The nourishment of your soul.

And everything in this world is designed to take that away from you. To tear it asunder.

Fight.

Control.

Survive.

The mother has needs, and her needs are first.

If you are loved wholly and completely, you can share that love with your children.

So take it. Take it all.

It's yours.

No apologies.

No excuses.

No responsibilities.

Everything you do is a sacrifice. You are the world's greatest martyr.

Your children will need a constant reminder of everything you have ever done for them.

This will serve as the foundation for rejecting accusations.

How could you be blamed for anything if all you've ever done was out of service to others?

Your behavior is justified in perpetuity.

Your actions are pure.

Your feelings and intuitions are never questioned.

You are the glue that holds the whole world together.

Sons under your guidance will grow up to be husbands.

Fathers to uphold the mothers.

Procreators to give children to the mothers.

Daughters will become wives.

Other Mothers.

A circle.

The Eternal Mother. Forever worshipped and adored.

Mother. Knows. Best.

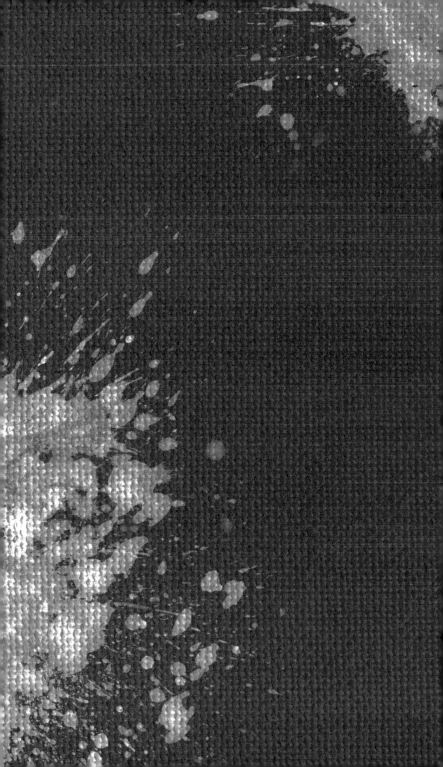

MOTHER BEAR
BY JACQUELINE WEST

Set me in the center of your stories.
Place me in the heart of the house
with ruffled curtains and geraniums,
bowls of porridge, wild cherry pie.

Tie on a bear-sized bonnet and apron.
Arrange skirts that nearly cover
my claws. Make me as docile as a toy,
broad and soft as a just-right bed.

Seat me in a bentwood chair to rock,
to crochet, to mend. Let children
picture themselves in my lap,
wrapped up tight in my strong arms.

Pretend that my love is sweet.
Pretend any golden-haired girl
who strode into my den would not
have been ripped to cherry-red shreds.

SO LOVELY IN THE DARK
BY JESSICA MCHUGH

Mama kept her favorite lipstick in a room without mirrors. They were unnecessary, she said, because of the pact.

When she told me the terms, they were meant as a warning, and they felt like one—austere secrets that created a fluttery sickness in me like a spider trapped in my ribcage—but as I aged, the terms felt right, even easy.

Especially at night.

I didn't dare tell her how deeply I longed to make the same pact she had, but it must've been obvious, as bold as the sun streaming through purple curtains the first time she led me into her bedroom. The channel of indigo light maximized the emptiness of the space like envy maximized mine. She encouraged me to embrace the beams of shifting lilac that day and still does, but they don't dazzle me the way they used to.

I suggested redecorating several times over the years—different curtains, a fresh coat of paint—but her response was always the same. She laughed away my suggestions like I was a babbling infant, and cradling my face, she said, "Purple is the color of royalty ... and decomposition. You'll learn to love it again."

And maybe she was right. The first time she showed me her favorite lipstick, I was instantly enamored by its dark violet sheen. And its decadent drugstore aroma captivated me so completely I thought to myself, *This is what purple smells like.*

It was all so obvious, so beautiful. Life made perfect sense in that room. Just Mama, her favorite lipstick, and me.

But it didn't stay simple for long. When she uncapped her lipstick a few days later, it had changed from its posh yet practical purple into a revolting ruby. I thought it a joke at first; somehow, Mama found a copy of the antique lipstick tube, with the same flecks of yellow and amethyst tarnish in the ravines of its twisted silver flesh, making it look just as bejeweled in the myrtle hue of her bedroom, and filled it with a scarlet lie.

But it wasn't a joke. She affirmed it wasn't a copy. It was the same lipstick, her one and only, her *favorite.*

The word was a wallop to the gut that emptied me of everything but an overwhelming feeling of betrayal. I was too young to know what betrayal felt like, yet it was all I could see, all I could taste, blistering and bitter as she swiped the impostor across her lips.

At that, she giggled in her carefree, condescending way and laid her hands upon my cheeks. Then the darkness came, whisking me away like a poisoned lullaby, and when I awoke alone, I forgot I was supposed to be angry.

The feeling of betrayal disappeared, too, and I soon became enamored by the lipstick's strange characteristics. By watching Mama's nightly rituals, I learned it was like the room, albeit with a wider spectrum. As she applied it and taunted me with air kisses before she left the house for her evening outings, it cycled pink and red, blue and black, like a bruise that refused to heal.

"What color would it be on *me*?" I asked, and she bopped me on the nose with a warble.

"You don't need to worry about that, darling. Your lips are so lovely, even in the dark."

She said it frequently to deflect my questions, I assume. Of which there were many, about the lipstick, the pact, and how on earth she took the room's colors with her when she left the house.

Mama shimmered as she strolled alone downtown, her lips neon pink against orchid skin. She never let me come along, but I saw her when I closed my eyes as if the streets of our gray city mirrored the circuits of my mind. It was torturous watching her walk the world so freely. I could've sworn I'd been that way once, but Mama said it was impossible. I'd always been there. In a way, I always would be, like Grammy and Papa before me. And as tempting as it was, I couldn't leave for the same reason I couldn't wear her favorite lipstick.

"It's too much of a risk, my darling. What you'd sacrifice … what I'd lose … and for what? Yes, it might accentuate your beauty, but only for a moment, like fireworks that bloom and fade but leave the sky forever scorched."

"It's really that bad?"

"Worse, I'm afraid." She shut the lipstick in its special box, tucked the box in its special drawer, and then sat next to me on the bed. "For a few moments of vibrance, your natural beauty will be stripped away. Not all at once, but eventually, with every coat and pucker, it will reduce you to ashes."

"But *you're* not ashes," I said. "You're the most beautiful person I've ever seen."

She thanked me with a giggle, but her gaze was aimed at Grammy and Papa in the corner, their faces shrouded in plum shadows. Both were slumped in their chairs, but only Papa's eyes were open, his chair rocking slightly from his foot intermittently kicking the floor.

Moving to the dressing table, she sighed. "The pact is a lifelong sacrifice, little one, and I will not see you consumed before your time. You're too exceptional."

Although those words rang through me from a young age, I was a preteen before they struck me odd enough to ask what she meant.

"Before my time? So, I'm going to be ashes no matter what?"

She painted a fresh coat onto the barrel of her bottom lip; it shone in iridescent jewel tones I swear smelled like all the best and worst parts of a carnival. The cloying scent made me swoon when she spoke.

"Yes, but it'll be worth it. Besides, you don't need this stuff." She dressed her mouth with a final swipe. "Your lips are already so lovely, even in the dark."

I tried to preserve my vibrancy the way she wanted, but the older I got, the more I thought about her favorite lipstick. What started as a splash of adoration became a whirling obsession in my body. With all its colors doubling, blending, and bursting like flame, and the aching pressure to hold it all in, I broke faster than I would've thought. Unable to contain my kaleidoscopic mania, I started giving it away.

So ravenous was my desire to feel sacrificial luxury upon my lips that I let people have their fill of my other parts. I knotted up strangers in my rich brown hair and let them drink my flesh like honey wine. I took my lovely mouth to midnight blue alleyways and sank the white moons of my fingernails into tumultuous umber seas, and never once in my rainbow debauchery did I feel consumed. Quite the opposite.

But despite my satisfaction, I returned from every encounter craving the lipstick even more. I spent entire nights awake, picturing how I'd sneak into Mama's room, quiet as a virus. I wouldn't even try to take it, just … *use* it … and let it use *me*. Sixty seconds, maybe less, to slide that slick aromatic paint over my mouth and know, at last, how it feels to be free.

Years passed while I explored those midnight fantasies, my skin still buzzing from the pale-yellow teeth I begged to carve into me hours before.

Mama kept her favorite lipstick in a tarnished silver box in a room without mirrors. She said if the sun wanted to dance with something reflective, it had no choice but to chase one of us.

"The chase keeps you alive. Be it for light, for love, or for …" The room went magenta for a moment, and she hummed as if catching a whiff of a delicious memory.

"For what, Mama?"

She rolled her gaze from me to Grammy, whose tremors had become so violent her knobby wrists sounded like a hammer missing a nail when they smacked the chair. Kneeling beside her, Mama held Grammy's hands and pressed her lips to the papery skin until the old woman stopped shaking. "For stillness," she whispered, her lips leaving a purple-black stain, like the tarnish consuming the silver box.

I wondered if Grammy ever wore Mama's lipstick. Or if it used to belong to her. Maybe it was passed from mother to daughter for generations, and Grammy delighted in the lip print on her hand.

But she looked so terrified of it. Her tremors had ceased temporarily, but only on the outside. Her eyeballs shivered between droopy lids. Her veins quaked beneath unnaturally still limbs. And behind her pale, shrunken lips and yellow teeth, her tongue twisted around a scream she'd never expel.

She and Papa were so frail by the end, it was a miracle the tremors didn't shudder their bony bodies to pieces. They were soft once, though. I recall the rosy silk of my grandmother's skin with better clarity than Mama's now. The more I think about it, the realer it seems, like I could reach into last week and touch Papa's red-blond stubble, scratchy against my fingertips but delicate as dandelion fluff against my cheek.

I hated seeing my grandparents in those chairs, their papery fingers weakly reaching out to me while Mama sat on the bed, hands folded neatly on her lap, watching in fascination. They wanted to hold. They wanted to comfort. They wanted to love me in a way Mama never could.

Now I think maybe they *did*.

We hardly talk about them anymore. Mama actually stopped before they were gone, so I did, too. Sometimes, I forgot they were still there, their bodies deteriorating so dramatically that, in the dim purple light, I couldn't distinguish them from their chairs until their eyes opened. Long after they passed, I still saw their broken shadows cast across that part of the room and caught myself waiting for those watery orbs to shine at me from the mulberry gloom.

The day they died, I—well, it's hard to remember now. I know I was there, but it's foggy, like so many things these days. I think they were in their chairs like always, mumbling, trembling, watching Mama's lipstick plump her pale mouth into an amaryllis bulb primed to bloom. Then, the chairs were empty, and all that remained was Mama, me, and my desire, which became increasingly harder to control. The struggle affected me so intensely that I no longer recognized the person I saw in rearview mirrors and dive bar bathrooms.

Mama changed, too. She wore the box's corrosion-like opera gloves. Her skin still cycled through purple hues, but the texture and shape also changed. Sometimes, she was soft and vibrant, and sometimes, she was as stretched and malformed as the deceptive shadows on the rocking chairs.

"A certain type of beauty makes the world go round," she said. "Even if it's a lie. The most beautiful things are kept in ugly boxes. That way, no one tries to steal their magic. That's what keeps them lush and generous, staying unseen … and untouched. Touch can be a ruinous thing. To the butterfly and the curious child with stolen color on their fingertips. And to be one and the same …" She ran a hand through my thinning hair and sighed. "That's what awaits you if you give in to your desire to steal from me."

I recoiled, wanting to both deny and confess to it by crumpling in shame, but I couldn't do either once her rigid hand moved to my cheek. Darkness bloomed like watercolors in my vision, but it didn't fill every space like usual, didn't box me in. Somewhere between reality and the timeless place her cradling sent me, I floated in the ether of her voice.

"This is growing up. This is the pact. It learns all your curves and colors, fears, and fetishes, and falls in love with the spark of power it'll transform into a blaze. Once that happens, there's no turning it off, no turning back. That's your life now. It's feeling like the last healthy vein in a world run by vampires. It's pride and fear and learning all too slowly that desire is the greatest force in this world—stronger than needing, stronger than having—and if someone's able to harness that energy, it spells destruction for everyone involved. From outside and within, they could control you, even occupy you. And as both legal tenant and squatter, they renovate as they see fit, with zero concern for frame or foundation."

I wanted to understand her so badly, if only to convince her not to send me back into the dark. But I couldn't. I was too ashamed to admit my desire didn't feel like that. I craved warmer, more malleable things and nights that wrapped their gratitude around me like a tomato vine embracing its stake. My yearning didn't fulfill me the way her lipstick would, but it made me feel alive, as vibrant as Mama after her nights downtown.

In reality, I was more like the lipstick *after* her evenings out: worn-down, chapped, and muddy gray. The first time I saw the cosmetic devoid of color, I thought it meant I'd finally outgrown my obsession. But as I slept, its colors entered me the way I entered the darkness brought on by Mama's touch, and as desire flared anew inside me, the lipstick flared, too. In its bruised silver box, its color and light returned as if I'd helped recharge its beauty.

I asked her once if someone could agree to the lipstick pact without knowing it. "Like, if you really wanted it, deep down, could you somehow agree without actually agreeing?"

One side of her mouth twitched up her cheek. "Well, of course, Violet. Otherwise, no one would agree."

Mama kept her favorite lipstick in the warped bottom drawer of a dark oak dressing table in a room without mirrors. What good were they anyway, she said as she rocked the drawer back into its nest. Real beauty couldn't be seen; it was something you felt, deep down, in cycles fertile and fallow, shifting like lipstick.

"Your favorite will be the same," she said. "If that's what you choose."

"I thought I didn't have a choice."

"To sacrifice your color according to the terms of the pact, no. But you can choose how you wield your power. When you find your favorite lipstick, you'll know what to do."

But at that moment, I knew I didn't want my own favorite. I wanted hers.

Like a sort of sweet torture, Mama held her lipstick aloft, twisted out a fresh inch of rose-gold gloss, and patted the spot beside her on the bed. As I scuttled to her, my heart fluttered with a feeling of lust and fate so strong it could only be hope. The seeds sown by my first glimpse of that forbidden cosmetic sprouted tendrils that tied me to every color on the spectrum of Mama's charity.

Then she capped it. It was like seeing the purple lipstick go red all over again. I was throttled, opened, and emptied by her betrayal. And I refused to accept it a moment longer.

Weeping, I threw myself at her feet and begged to wear it. Just a little. Just once.

She pouted. "But your lips are—"

"Don't say it! Please, just make it stop. I don't want to feel this way anymore."

She stared at me in shock, then at the empty gray chairs rocking under the weight of memory. I hated those chairs, hard

11

and cobwebbed in misery, but they looked comfortable now, the seats softer, the wood cool and smooth as brass.

Or maybe I was just tired. My back ached terribly. My legs, too.

"Are you finished?" she asked.

I shook my head with a whimper. "Why are you doing this to me?"

Reaching out a lavender hand, she smiled. "Because your lips are so lovely, even in the dark."

When she touched my cheek, her fingers seemed to pass through my face, into my neck and chest, and out the other side of me, but not before grabbing what she needed.

As light and form returned, faint figures appeared, calling me closer, calling me deeper, calling me theirs. But even then, they only ever found me at the end of the road. Like the terms of the pact, like finally wearing Mama's lipstick. I wanted to ask why there was no journey, no discovery, no struggle to find the light. But I had no voice where she sent me, only breath that ran out faster and faster, and when the sound of the juddering drawer cut through the din of my suffocation, it opened like a promise in my body, pleading for me to trade royalty for decomposition. It's a plea I answered time and time again, but that time, the last time, I gave it a resounding "yes."

Mama keeps her favorite lipstick in the longing of a little girl lost in a room without mirrors.

I've agreed to the terms. I'll sacrifice whatever it takes. I'll enter the pact gleefully and walk the city streets with my mouth open, a strong woman like Mama, for as long as I can until we're both ashes.

I tell her this, and my knees instantly buckle. I need to sit down, just for a moment.

Mama is a stalk of lavender wheat, thin but thriving as she helps me to a rocking chair. My bones creak and crackle as she lowers me, and when she kisses me on the forehead, I feel the wetness of her lipstick like an open wound.

I whisper, trembling, "I'm sorry, Mama. I'm not lovely anymore. I'm pale and empty and so very confused. The pact didn't strip my color. I did. I gave it away."

When she tilts her head, her face sinks into itself, and the purple light finds new canyons in which to cast its shadows. She lifts my chin with a bony finger, her expression more forgiving than expected. "Oh, my sweet little Violet ... of course you did."

I struggle to lift my head, so she helps me, centering it between my shoulders as she purrs, "Thank you, child. You've given me so much. I knew you were special, but I never expected all this. The others desired what they couldn't have but didn't want to live and die for it as you did. The power you generated with that hunger was like none I've felt in all my years in this world. You've kept me alive far longer, but you also made me *feel* more alive than I have in ages. You're so lovely, even now, pale, and empty in the dark. I cherish you for that. But our time as mother and daughter is almost over, your strength is almost gone, and I need to find another source."

There's a strange fog in the room now. She floats through it to the dressing table, opens the broken drawer, removes the tarnished box, and bends to the lid so dramatically her spine appears to unfold in spikes all the way up her back. She looks like a piece of broken scaffolding struggling under the weight of the box, which she opens with a labored grunt.

"Mama …"

My voice is a faint alien thing that barely tumbles off my tongue. She hears me but doesn't turn until her lips are fully dressed. The lipstick softens her up a bit, but she's mostly cheekbones and melancholy as she glides to me again, the moist purple pillar twisted to its limit and extended to my face. The nearer it draws to my lips, the brighter it grows, and the more I can taste its creamy poison through scent alone. I try to close the distance between us, but I'm shaking too much to steer my body.

She exhales a chuckle, and when she presses the moist purple stick to my lips, my tremors stop. The room is clear again, and I am a child entering the lilac space for the first time.

"I want to see myself, Mama! A mirror, please! Any mirror!"

But then she kisses me, and I feel the makeup drain from my lips into hers. My voice is an earthquake again, and my bones pound the chair as I shiver.

Smiling fondly, she says, "Oh, Violet, *you were* the mirror. You reflected everything—desire, beauty, color, death—and from that, you generated the power the lipstick demanded. Armed with that tool, you allowed me to hunt comfortably these last few weeks, unashamed and aglow. I won't forget you for that. Even when you forget me."

"I would never forget you, Mama."

"You will. You'll forget me the way you forgot your real parents. Your home. Your name."

She twists on the cap, places her favorite lipstick in its tarnished box, and closes it inside the broken drawer. Bathed in magenta light, she bends to me in the chair. "If you're still here when I get back, don't be afraid of what you'll hear. It's the way of the pact."

She touches my cheek, but the darkness doesn't come— only the gray dust of the years I lost in that room. I think I might be lost in it forever, that Mama will never return.

But she does. Through the fog, I see her enter the room and open her arms to the purple light. A small figure twitches behind her, and she turns with an encouraging cheer.

"Go on. Embrace it," she says, but the little girl toddling into the room shakes her head.

"I don't like purple."

Mama hums. "That's okay. You'll learn to love it, Violet." Smiling at me through the ashes, she says, "Just like your Grammy."

ALMONDS
BY LISA KRÖGER

Maddie knew the exact distance from the turnoff on the turnpike to the start of her mother's driveway. She didn't know how far in miles or feet. Nor did she know it in minutes or seconds.

But she did know that she had just enough time to pull out her lipstick from her purse, apply the color to her lips, blot, apply again, check herself in the mirror, and pop her lips together three times. Then, she'd put the makeup back in her purse just as she turned her car into the driveway.

Maddie knew this because she did this every time she visited her mother, without fail. So she could avoid the dreaded—

"You look tired." Her mother stood aside in the doorway so Maddie could enter.

Maddie tossed her keys and purse on the table in the foyer. "Thanks, Mom," she said.

"Hey, hon," her mother said, holding out her arms for a hug. "Don't take it that way, please." She held her daughter at a distance, her hands squeezing Maddie's shoulders, and looked her up and down. "I'm just worried about you. That's all."

Then, she pulled Maddie in for a hug, and for one moment, Maddie let herself melt into her mother, smelling her perfume,

Red Door by Elizabeth Arden, the same thing she'd worn for decades. Red Door mixed with the stale smell of cigarettes. There was some comfort to be had in consistency.

Then, Maddie felt her mother pat her hands along her back.

"Have you put on weight?"

Maddie pulled away. "Jesus, Mom."

Her mother shrugged. "What? You carry it well, at least." She looked down at her manicure. "I never could carry that kind of weight. I don't have the build for it. But you—you take after your father's side."

Maddie closed her eyes, took in a big breath. This week was going to be a mistake.

Maddie unpacked her suitcase in what had once been her childhood bedroom. Her double bed was still there, but her dresser had been replaced by a behemoth treadmill. Maddie folded her clothes and stacked them on the machine. Her mother wouldn't be using it after her surgery anyway, and Maddie knew she wouldn't touch the thing. She slid her suitcase under the bed and joined her mother in the kitchen, where the table was laid with two plates.

Her mother stood at the stove, a boiling stock pot in front of her.

"Is it okay for you to be having food?" Maddie said, walking to the fridge. She opened it, found a half-drunk bottle of chardonnay, and pulled it out.

"I'm on all liquids after midnight. Water only. But the doctor said I can have a light dinner tonight." She nodded to a cabinet just behind Maddie. "Glasses are in there. Ice is in the freezer. Use the tray, though. The ice maker is broken again. I don't know how I'm going to fix it."

"I'm sure it's still under warranty. When did you buy it?"

"Last year." Her mother shook her head furiously as Maddie reached into the cabinet and removed a stemless wine glass. "Not those. Those are for red. Use the smaller ones with the stem."

Maddie exhaled deeply. Then she grabbed the stemmed glass and poured herself a chardonnay.

"Leave room for ice."

"I don't need it, Mom, it's fine."

"It'll melt as you drink. Always helps me drink a lot less."

Maddie's mother microwaved leftover boiled chicken breasts and opened a can of asparagus. They ate in silence. Well, her mother ate while Maddie picked at her food with her fork, mostly just moving it around the plate. If her mother noticed, she didn't say anything. It occurred to Maddie that maybe her mother was even a little proud of her daughter for showing such restraint around food.

Later that night, Maddie was predictably hungry. Her mother found her standing in front of the pantry.

"I always grab a handful of almonds if I get peckish at night." As her mother spoke, she picked a piece of imaginary lint off her shoulder to avoid looking at Maddie.

"Mom, you don't have food." Maddie looked over the cans of vegetables, the jars of olives, the Costco-sized container of raw almonds. "I'll go shopping tomorrow night once I get you home and resting."

"I just went shopping, Madison."

Maddie smiled. "You will be in bed with a large patch over your eye."

"Don't get old," her mother said. "I don't recommend it. It's horrible."

Maddie looked at her mother, petite and thin, in her large black-rimmed glasses. She looked so small and old—more frail than the last time Maddie was here.

A little bit later, Maddie sat in her room, an enormous tub of almonds in bed beside her. Her mother cautioned her to only eat a handful, but Maddie had only heard that as a challenge. She was nothing if not petty. Following her mother's cataract surgery tomorrow, she'd head to the store and get some real food. In the meantime, almonds. She dug into the tub, pulled out a large mass of nuts, and shoved them into her mouth, the latest Stephen King book in her other hand. As it turned out, Maddie was not good at juggling because as soon as she turned the page, the tub of almonds fell from her hands, sending almonds skittering across the floor.

"Shit." She put down her book and got to her hands and knees, scooping up the almonds. They were everywhere. Under the bed, across the room, everywhere. Most of it proved to be an easy cleanup, except for under the treadmill, too narrow of a space for Maddie to sweep her hand under. It took a few good pushes, but eventually, she got the treadmill moved just enough to finish cleaning the floor, which—

"What is that?"

In front of her was a hole in the floor, previously hidden by the treadmill. Perfectly round, maybe five inches in diameter. Maddie got close enough to peer down. It was deep and dark, at least a foot if she had to guess, which didn't make sense, as her bedroom was on the second floor, directly above the living room. How deep were the floors?

Curiosity took over, and Maddie grabbed her phone, using the flashlight to get a better look. With the light, she could see that the whole was deeper than her original estimate. Even stranger, it was round the entire way down, more of a tube or tunnel than a hole. Maddie looked around for something she could drop down. Her gaze landed on the almonds.

With her phone for a light, she dropped one almond. It fell and fell until the light no longer hit. Maddie guessed that the hole must be deep because she never heard the sound of the almond hitting the bottom.

If there was a bottom.

Maddie shivered. Why had she thought that? Of course, it must have a bottom—right?

Nausea swept over her, and she moved to the bed, not bothering to push the treadmill back into place. She didn't want to think about that hole anymore—except that she did. It was the only thing rolling around in her head, no matter how hard she tried to think about anything else.

Maddie thought about her mother and how she hadn't wanted to come home. That made her a bad daughter. She knew that. But her sister had kids of her own, a husband, a life. Who would take care of the kids? No, she couldn't afford a babysitter. And their father had left many years ago. Their mother was alone, something that Maddie had said many times in therapy was the old woman's own fault. But this was different. Her mother really did need her, and Maddie couldn't say no.

Would she be a terrible person to admit that she almost hadn't come? Or that she thought maybe her mother's failing eyesight would be a blessing? That maybe her mother seeing her oldest daughter blurry was better than seeing her crystal clear—that maybe the lack of clarity would keep the criticism away.

Maddie's mother had been a beauty when she was younger. More than once, they'd been stopped in public, people commenting on how her mother looked. "Do you know who you look like?" It was almost always some movie star. And it wasn't a surprise, with her mother's dark curls and emerald eyes. But they slowly stopped; Maddie didn't remember when exactly. It wasn't as if it was something that they marked with a little scratch on the calendar or even something they talked about after. Maddie only noticed it had stopped when she was a preteen, and someone turned to her mother and said, "Do you know—"

Her mother smiled, looked down, her practiced modesty, and said, "Yes, I've heard that a lot."

At the same time, the man was saying, "That you have a beautiful daughter."

Maddie didn't remember what else was said. Only that her mother had pressed her lips in one thin line and pulled Maddie away. Later in the car, Maddie said, "That was nice of him to say that." It was the first time she had heard someone not related to her—not a teacher, not an adult who was obliged to be complimentary—say something so nice to her.

"People say we are pretty, Maddie," her mother replied. "I personally have never seen what they must see."

Maddie never brought it up again.

Now, so many years later, Maddie lay in bed, with her mother sleeping downstairs, and wondered if that statement had been the one-time slip of her mother's mask, showing the soft underside of self-consciousness. Or if it was a slight dig to her daughter, making sure Maddie knew exactly how her mother felt about her.

Even now, she didn't know.

Maddie tried to close her eyes, to take a deep breath, to try and find sleep.

It wouldn't come.

Her mother slept unbothered downstairs. And she was up here, reliving every moment of her childhood. Maddie had always had insomnia. It had plagued her since childhood.

"Oh, you were awful," her mother had said once, a few years ago. "Never slept, up at all hours of the night. Even as an older child, not a baby, mind you. I would've given you up if it had been socially acceptable to do something like that."

"You gave away my dog." It was the only thing that Maddie could think to say.

Her mother had laughed. "That damn animal dug up all of my flower bulbs from the back bed. It never did grow hardly a thing even after I sent him away."

Her mother had been smoking a Virginia Slim, taking long drags as she spoke.

"Oh, don't look at me like that, Madison," she said. "You hated that dog, too."

Maddie didn't. But she also didn't say anything else about it.

She opened her eyes again, stared at the ceiling. She wouldn't survive a week with her mother, not even if her mother wore eye coverings and was medicated. This house was stifling.

And then there was that hole.

She wondered if her mother knew it was there. She wondered how long it had been there. She wondered who had put it there.

Or if it had simply grown there, like a cancer.

Maddie's brain gnawed at that word: grown.

She imagined that it must have begun small, like a black dot, and spread. She could see the picture in her mind: a dot like a freckle becoming a pockmark, becoming a divot, becoming a hole, becoming a tunnel.

The image grew until her legs twitched at the very thought of it. She rolled over and stared at the mess she'd made in the room—the furniture pushed to the side, the pile of almonds.

The hole.

Maddie slid from the bed to the floor, inching toward it.

It looked like it had grown by maybe an inch or an inch and a half. But that was in her mind. It had to be.

Still, she picked up an almond and tossed it in, just as she had before.

She watched as it fell into the darkness. Again, she didn't hear it hit the bottom.

This time, though, she saw small tendrils of smoke curling up from the darkness.

Cigarette smoke. No mistaking that smell.

Maddie watched, worried for just a second that maybe there was a fire that could spread. But she relaxed once she realized the wispy puffs wafted away into nothing.

In front of her, the perimeter of the hole stretched. It shuddered as if cold.

Maddie's eyes grew wide, her skin cold, as she realized it was growing. Another inch, at least.

Now, it seemed to be at least seven or eight inches across.

Hands shaking, Maddie reached for her phone, turning on the flashlight once again. There was no doubt about it: the hole had changed. It was bigger now, and the perimeter was no longer perfectly round but more organic.

Like a breathing thing.

Maddie shivered. She shouldn't think things like that. The odor of stale cigarettes still hung in the air, and she felt as if she might retch.

Still, she kept looking inside, which had changed, too. The hole had now changed in color, a beige that could only be described as flesh.

Skin. The hole in the floor that went down to nowhere was covered in skin.

It shook as if vibrating. And then shuddered another wisp of cigarette smoke directly into Maddie's face.

Breathing. It was breathing.

She coughed and waved her hand in front of her face, a reflex. And she thought she heard a laugh from deep within.

I would've given you away if I could.

And then, she dropped the phone. It simply slid from her hand, and she watched as it dropped deep down, the hole slowly swallowing the small light.

Maddie reacted from pure instinct and thrust her hand into the hole after her phone. Instead, she felt the soft and pliant mounds of flesh and nothing more. She pulled back her hand with a jerk.

She sat back, her heart beating a fast rhythm against her chest, and pressed her palms against her face. The growing hole in the floor didn't make any logical sense, yet here she was looking at it. She couldn't believe how stupid she had been, dangling her phone over that thing. What did she expect would happen? Now, she had lost her phone to who knows where.

Then, an idea dawned.

Her phone had tracking.

"Jesus, thank you. Or Steve Jobs." She went through her bag and pulled out her laptop. It should—

"Yes!" She could use Find My Phone, and there it was. A blinking blue dot in a circle. It didn't have much accuracy, but she could tell it was here in the house. It wasn't gone.

Placing the laptop on the bed, far from the hungry mouth in the floor, Maddie took a deep breath and scooted closer to the hole, rolling up her right-hand sleeve as she did.

She squeezed her eyes shut and plunged her hand in, doing it fast, forcefully, before she could talk herself out of it. She lowered her body to the floor until she fished into the hole nearly up to shoulder. The hole had grown wider, and she felt around until her fingers grazed what felt like the top of her phone. She reached deeper, straining her fingertips.

A puff of smoke rose, carrying a laugh on its hazy tendrils. *The weight looks good on you. You carry it well.*

She ignored the voice, which was maybe in her head or maybe within the thing on the floor. She wasn't sure. But she was sure that she almost had her phone. She just had to reach a little bit more.

Her fingertips pushed it down just a bit.

She strained.

And then she felt the hole pushing back against her. She could feel the fleshiness, now wet with a viscous material. It made a sucking sound as she moved her fingers around in it. The sound itself surprised her, and Maddie's reflex was to pull her hand up.

But she couldn't. The hole was closing now, around her arm.

The skin of the hole breathed in and out. Maddie could feel the motion with each inhale and exhale.

She panicked, trying with all her might to pull her hand back, but she couldn't, no matter how hard she pulled.

Maddie thought to scream, but instead, pulled once again, blood rushing to her face and tears welling in her eyes. She used her left hand to get leverage, but stopped when it felt as if her own skin at her shoulder was ripping away, bone popping from joint.

She screamed, but she only heard a whimper in her ears, as if the sound echoed from a place far away.

The next morning, Maddie's mother came to wake her daughter but found no Maddie. Instead, she found that the bed had been made, the laptop closed on top of the duvet, and her clothes neatly folded on the treadmill, which had returned to its original place.

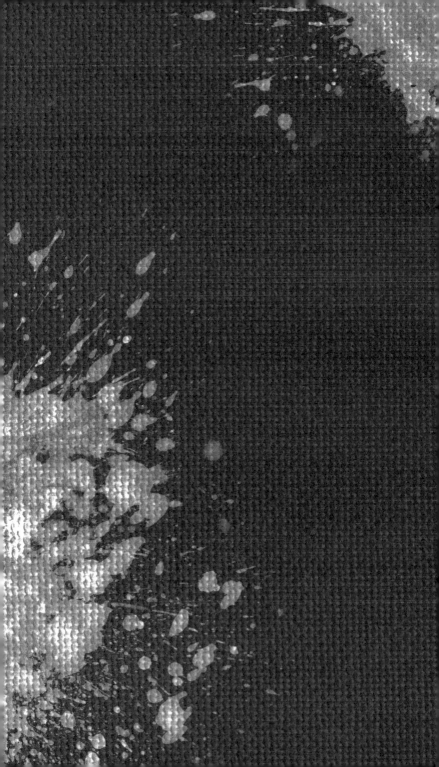

JUST LIKE YOUR MOTHER
BY N. J. EMBER

She has her mother's teeth so she knows how to consume.
One of Medea's children—nearly eaten in the womb.
From biblical to umbilical, unbroken is this tie.
She doesn't have her mother's smile and so,
she can't detect her lies.

She doesn't have her mother's eyes,
but mother's temper lives all too well
deep inside her skin and bones,
on a tether so no one can tell.

Mother said that she must break her
in order to build her up, so that she's strong.
Trauma gifted from mother tongue to mother tongue,
each generation keeps getting it wrong.

In the blood there lives a curse of women beaten black and blue
and if you're really lucky Mother will gift back to you.
Never mind how you're born from between her thighs,
to her you're nothing but a liar.

But you don't have her eyes.

OH, WHAT A TANGLED WEB
BY TANYA PELL

They don't have the milk.

Marnie stares into the cooler, the glass foggy and smudged from fingerprints and cheap cleaning products. She can see the spirals from the half-hearted wipe-down it was given some time in the last week. That pattern had been different the last time she was in. Zigzags instead of swirls.

Her reflection is little more than a silhouette that blocks the aisle behind her—a dark, no-faced phantom framed by packed shelves of stale snack cakes and leathery jerky. Messy hair, oversized coat, boots laced haphazardly. The glass distortion gives her extra limbs, fuzzy and warped. If she had tracing paper, she could sketch her outline to baste and embroider later onto cloth. She could make a substitute for Marnie, picking careful colors of thread. Brighter colors. More palatable. A better Marnie. One her mother might approve of.

One that could get the milk.

Marnie opens the door once more—*third time's the charm*—and scans each shelf for the fucking milk while the cool air freezes the moisture on her eyeballs and the hum of the unit fills her ears like a taunt.

She lets the door shut with a *whoosh*, hand gripping the rubber and metal handle. Maybe if she looks again. Whole. Cream-O-Land. That's what she needs. What mother demands. It has to be there, right? Surely it is. It's probably right in front of her, and she's just not seeing it. She could have hundreds of eyes and still not—

"Excuse me."

The exasperated voice nearly startles Marnie into dropping the basket holding her meager shopping. A woman is standing to the side, a frown on her face, brows plucked thin, the remnants meeting in a V of displeasure between her eyes. Her hair is hidden under a silky cap, the overhead lights reflecting off the sheen. Her eyes are tired, harried, and she wears wrinkled scrubs under a heavy puffer coat. She clutches the hand of a little boy, his tiny fingers holding tight. He presses into the woman's hip, nervous or frightened, seeking the safety of his mother as he is faced with a strange woman.

"Can I get by?" the woman asks briskly, and Marnie wonders how long she has been waiting while Marnie tries to conjure the milk into existence.

"I'm sorry," Marnie mutters, stepping back until she hits an end display, metal prongs holding packets of mixed nuts digging into her back. Ashamed, Marnie turns down the candy aisle, a dark shadow among the colorful wrappers. She'd bought a bunch of cheap suckers for Halloween and left them in a bowl outside the door for trick-or-treaters. The next morning, the bowl was still full. She couldn't even give away free candy properly.

Her mother had laughed and laughed.

At the thought, Marnie drags the corner of her upper lip between her teeth and bites down till the pain has her seeing stars, and blood coats her tongue. She sucks at the wound, the already bruised and swollen skin protesting. A painful, distracting habit.

The woman hurries past to the checkout, dragging her son along as he glances anxiously at Marnie. Marnie doesn't attempt a smile, knowing her teeth are stained red, thin strips of skin from her lips clinging to her incisors. She swallows the warm blood, the taste of pennies over her palate, and turns down another aisle, avoiding the counter till the bleeding stops.

She throws bread, a few cans of cat food, and some tuna into her basket. She'd make tuna sandwiches for lunch. Maybe she should pick up a different milk. Mother might not know the difference.

She would know.

Marnie sighs and looks out the smoky gas station window, rubbing at a sore spot between her shoulders. Her back hurts all the time now. Too much time bent over, needle in hand in the darkness of their apartment, pinning and quilting. Fingers pricked and knuckles sore. She flexes her hands inside the gloves she'd knitted last year.

A truck is pulled up along the back fence, its red rig dusty and covered in highway salt. The driver is probably taking a nap in his bunk or grabbing a burger at the greasy spoon next door. For a second, she fantasizes about walking out, the tiny bell over the door ringing in celebration of her bravery, and asking the driver for a ride. Maybe she'll do that. Just hitch rides with truckers who might lie and tell her she's pretty for a few miles.

She's not sure she would mind the lies. Maybe pretty lies are better than ugly truths.

She will ride to the next gas station and then the next, all of them different and all of them the same. The same clerks selling the same candy bars and condoms, only they'll have new faces and wear different name tags. Jordan will turn into Carla, who will turn into Navi, who will become Reagan. The cities will have different names, but the stations will all smell of fumes, and their fluorescent lights will buzz. She will become a ghost, haunting the waypoints for weary travelers, the liminal spaces between home and adventure. And she'll have neither.

It sounds so nice to be nobody. Well, she already is nobody, but it would be lovely to be nobody else. A different nobody.

But she is *this* nobody, and she needs to get back. She has left Mother for too long.

Hurrying to the counter, the frayed edges of dreams of independence and escape floating away like spider silk, she passes item after item to Jordan. He is strangely silent today. He finally looks up into her face, and something in his eyes is different. "Lotto ticket today?"

Her head bobbles in relief at the acknowledgment. "Yes!" she says too eagerly. "You're out of Mother's milk," she blurts out, just to hear him speak to her. Just so she knows she is still there. "The whole milk. Cream-O-Land."

"Oh. Maybe tomorrow?"

Marnie winces, feeling as if she has been critical when it was only meant to be an observation. She isn't good at this. At conversation. At anything beyond her needle and thread. Mother tells her so. "I'm sorry. I mean, that's fine."

Jordan clears his throat. "I'll—uh—need to see your license. For the ticket."

"Oh. Sure," Marnie agrees, confused. She's never had to do that before, has she? She fumbles in her purse for her wallet and thumbs out her old driver's license. The picture is old, the card expired.

Jordan looks at it for a moment before he passes it back. As she slips it into its plastic shield, he writes something down on a bit of paper. He gives her the total, and she hands him her credit card. Then, it is all a regular routine; him placing her purchases into a plastic bag before handing her the card and the lotto ticket. She thanks him, takes her bag, and leaves.

On the sidewalk, she pulls up the hood of her coat, the new, furry trim tickling her face. Marnie's head turns to the ground beside the ice cooler and the stainless-steel bowls filled with cat food. The food is untouched, brown, red, and tan pellets, probably frozen. There used to be so many cats, having litters in the boxes meant for recycling by the back dumpster. Jordan fed them the expired food from the store. He said they kept the rodents away. He said he felt sorry for them.

No cats today. No paw marks in the filthy snow.

Marnie burrows as deep into her coat as she can, picking her way across the icy lot toward home. She passes old benches, years of graffiti baked into the wood. A bus stop is much the same, grimy, and covered in bird shit, cigarette butts, and posters for missing pets, their edges curling inward from damp and wind. *Have you seen this dog?*

Up the cracked steps and into the stairwell, the light that filters in is dreamy at the entrance, dust motes dancing in the air. Another liminal space. Between the cold sunlight outside and the poorly heated hell above. Marnie grips the rail hard and forces herself upward into the dark, already anticipating her welcome home.

She rounds the third flight of stairs, breath short from both fear and minimal exercise. A baby is crying in apartment 3A. It is a hungry cry, Marnie thinks. But not for food. For attention. For love. Marnie knows that cry well. The wails quiet as Marnie ascends higher, and Marnie pictures a loving, doting mother reaching down and gathering the child up, cooing. The baby has Marnie's face.

Outside their apartment, Marnie wipes her feet over and over on the old mat, trying to get any remaining salt and slush off her boots. Delaying. It is more with resignation than courage that she finally opens the door into the quiet dark and slips inside.

Marnie toes off her boots and slips out of her coat and gloves, wincing at each crinkle of the plastic bag as she shifts it from hand to hand. She hangs the coat on the wall next to the net and scarf she'd crotched by hand. She'd forgotten to wear the scarf. She looks down the darkened tunnel toward the door to the living room, feeling the presence there like a slumbering dragon before she tiptoes to the kitchen, afraid to disturb the silence and awaken her mother's wrath.

It makes her nervous to come home to silence. It feels like waiting for a blow to land or a bomb to detonate.

It feels like a trick.

She avoids the black trash bags leaking their contents onto the floor, the old, yellowed laminate sticky and brown. Flies buzz here and there, drawn to the spillage. A box of fly paper sits open on top of cans of tuna and cat food. Marnie should hang another ribbon from the ceiling and take down some of the old. Many are dusty and gray, the tiny black bodies of the flies piled so thick she can no longer see the golden tape. The spiders in the corners are well-fed, their intricate, lacey webs cluttered with iridescent, squirming bodies.

She is glad she doesn't have to open the fridge since there is no milk. She tries to keep it clean, but it gets so hard. She cannot take the world apart each day and recreate it new like the spider does. She tries to take out the spoiled things a little at a time, quietly. Mother demands so much more these days, but Marnie can't always get to them in time and—

"Marnie."

She feels sick at the sound of her name in that dry, angry voice. She steels herself, ready to get it over with. "They didn't have your milk, Mama."

The judgment is swift, a goddess displeased with a lack of offering. "Stupid girl."

"Jordan said maybe tomorrow. I can go—"

"Oh! Jordan, is it? That why you're taking so long? Bet you didn't even look for the milk. Too busy with Jordan."

The blood rushes to Marnie's face, filling each capillary to bursting. "Mama, Jordan isn't interested in me."

"Nobody would be. Can't even get milk."

The space closes in around her, and Marnie has to put a hand on the counter to steady herself. She does not want to have this conversation again. Any conversation again. She wants to scream that her mother doesn't even drink the milk anyway! That it just goes sour and rotten like everything else!

"I'll get more of everything tomorrow, Mother."

Her mother ignores her. "There's work to be done."

So soon? But Marnie is already flexing her fingers, threading the needle in her head, feeling the pierce and give and pull as if she has already begun. When she's working, there is quiet. Her mother gives her this modicum of respect, at the least. "Okay, Mama."

She steps out of the kitchen and down an adjacent hall to the bathroom, fumbling for the light switch. The naked bulbs above the mirror glow too bright, and Marnie avoids her face in the mirror. She doesn't want to see the haunted eyes drawn down by heavy lines and bruised circles. Or the mangled, broken skin of her lip, shredded by her own teeth. The earlier bite is still fresh, and her cheek feels warm. Infection?

A frosted bottle of alcohol is next to her toothbrush, and she dabs some on a few pieces of toilet paper before pressing it to her lip with a catlike hiss. The sting is like a brand, and her entire face spasms. God, it hurts!

The sink is a mess of bottles, paper towels, and gloves. Marnie tosses an empty container of bleach from the last cleanup into the tub, where it clatters about with the rest while a spider watches from behind the showerhead. She should have restocked at the QT. Never mind. Tomorrow.

She leans against the sink, tongue probing the inside of her face, and tries to mentally gather her supplies. She'll need to see how big the job is. Does she have enough supplies? She's running low. Stock is hard to come by, like the milk.

Tomorrow. She'll check again tomorrow.

A knock on the door.

Marnie starts, sending a new wave of pain through her face. They never have visitors.

She hurries back down the hall, passing the living room, and hears her mother call out. "Marnie!"

"In a minute, Mother," Marnie whispers. "Someone is here."

It's probably the super about the smell or the leak in the bathroom again. Someone probably complained. But it isn't Mr. Covey in the hall when Marnie peers out into the hallway. It is two uniformed officers, a man, and a woman, their noses still red from the cold. The man speaks first. "Mrs. Chearna?"

"Miss," Marnie corrects breathily through the crack in the door.

He nods. "Miss Chearna, we'd like to talk to you about an incident at the QT down the street?"

"I don't know what you mean."

Her mother's voice is sharp and furious. "Marnie! You're letting the heat out!"

"We'd like to discuss something captured on the QT security camera with you," the female officer says.

"I'm sorry. Who are you?"

The woman apologizes sweetly. "I'm so sorry. I'm Officer Clark, and this is Officer Morgan. As I was saying, we'd like to talk to you about a video, so if you could come with us to the station? Won't take long."

"No. No, I'm sorry." Marnie blinks, beseeching the officers. "I can't. My mother is here and needs me. I do everything for her."

"She's useless!" her mother calls, the strength in her voice bellying Marnie's suggestions of a frail, old woman.

Marnie moans, mortified, twisting the knob in her grip.

"Absolutely worthless. Just look at the state of things!"

"You won't give me a chance to clean! You always have me working!" Marnie snaps back, her face scarlet with shame.

"I have you fixing your mistakes!"

The officers look at each other, communicating silently, probably thinking she is a terrible daughter.

A fly buzzes by her ear, and she swats at it impatiently. "I'm sorry. You see, they didn't have Mother's milk at the QT this morning."

Her mother cackles cruelly, missing nothing. "Tell them what you did!"

Angry tears fill her eyes. "Mother, please! I've said I was sorry over and over!"

Clark clears her throat. With her hair pulled back in a tight ponytail, her eyes appear larger. They are big and brown and kind. Doe eyes, Marnie thinks they are called. "You do frequent the QT down the street?"

"Did I forget to pay this morning? I bought some bread and a few things. And a lotto ticket! For Mother. Was the card declined?" Marnie laughs, but the sound is hollow. "Well, why didn't Jordan say something? I could have paid with—"

"My money! Depositing my disability and social security checks every month won't even get me my milk!"

"They didn't *have* it!" she screams into the darkened apartment, spittle flying, bubbles popping on her swollen bottom lip. She turns back, flustered. "I'm sorry. I'll make it right."

Again, the mocking laugh. "You've not been able to do anything right your entire life!"

"Shut up, shut up, shut up," Marnie says through gritted teeth.

Morgan shakes his head. "We didn't say anything, ma'am."

Marnie is feeling feverish. She is probably coming down with something, and how would she get what her mother needs then? It is already so hard. "Not you. I'm sorry. What was it you wanted? I need to pay Jordan?"

Clark looks around. "Would you prefer we step inside? Maybe we can sort it out here."

"Oh. I suppose."

Then she shuts the door behind them, the hallway going dark. The man coughs into the elbow of his coat. She hopes he isn't sick. But the woman's nose is twitching. The smell, then. Marnie forgets about the smell. She is so used to it.

Another apology forms on her broken lips. Her entire life is one apology after the next. A patchwork quilt of apologies that began with "I'm sorry for being born." Her tongue stitches the next in the pattern: "I'm sorry. About the smell. I had the windows open and the heat off for so long, but it was too cold. I couldn't sew. My fingers ..."

She holds up her hands in the darkened corridor. Scratches mar the pale skin. Off-brand bandages wrapped around knuckles and fingertips, their edges fraying, some stained the color of rust. One digit is swollen, angry. Marnie is getting early arthritis in that hand, and she'd not been as careful as she might. Two needle sharp pricks and now this.

"Those do look pretty bad, Marnie," Morgan says, breathing through his mouth. But she likes the concern. Like she is somebody.

Marnie traces a few thin red lines with the tip of one calloused finger, feeling the rough, jagged scabs knitted over torn flesh. Skin cells were marvelous seamstresses. They sewed themselves together without thread or needle, barely leaving a seam. Though some wounds, Marnie knows, will never knit properly.

"Did your cat scratch you?"

"I don't have a pet." Marnie just has Mother. It would have been nice to have something that loved her. But she wouldn't have been able to bear a pet's disapproval, too.

"That's right." Mother's voice high and trilling. "Complain. Tell them how awful I was to you. Tell them what a monster I was. And then it'll be my turn."

"Mother, just *stop*! Why won't you just stop?"

"Did you say your mother was here with you, Marnie?" Clark asks.

"She's always here. She can't leave." Marnie giggles. She shoves her bandaged fingers against her mouth, the sound foreign and blasphemous in the gloom and sadness of the little apartment. "I'm sorry. Yes. I take care of her. There's just us."

Clark offers a thin smile. "What a lovely thing to be a caretaker."

"Oh, you take such good care of me, don't you, Marnie?" her mother snickers.

"It's not lovely," Marnie snaps, eyes beginning to spill over. "It's exhausting, and she hates me. She's always hated me. I thought I could fix her. Make her where she wouldn't hate me anymore."

Morgan coughs uncomfortably, but Clark just reaches out a hand and pats Marnie's shoulder. "I'm so sorry. I wasn't trying to upset you."

Marnie shakes her head, wiping at her eyes. "No, I'm sorry. I'm just a bit of a mess today, is all. And Mother says I have more work to do. Stitching and such."

Clark chuckles. "I can't sew on a button. I bet your work is lovely."

Something foreign blossoms in Marnie's chest. It is so out of place that she doesn't even recognize it as pride. "Would you like to see?"

Morgan looks dubious, but Clark looks pleasantly surprised. "We'd love to."

Marnie grins, blood running thinly down to smear across her lips as she ushers them deeper in. She points to several embroideries in various grubby frames. "I did these. Mother always liked florals."

Clark nods at the bouquets and landscapes of thread. "Lovely. Do you sell them? Have an Etsy shop or something?"

"Mother says nobody would buy anything I make." She points to a quilt hanging from two compression knobs. Each square contains an eye, all the irises cut from different swatches: spotted blue, cheetah print, swirling galaxy. It had been something new to try. Something challenging and creative.

How Mother had hated it.

"That's really cool," Morgan says, sounding surprised. He leans closer and then shifts from foot to foot. "They follow you. Like the Mona Lisa."

The praise will be the death of her, but Marnie decides she will be glad of it. "This," she gestures to a tapestry on the opposite wall, "I finished a month or so ago."

The piece is unlike anything else she ever attempted. Dark and strange, a mixture of embroidery and quilting and needlework. It is huge and seems to suck all the ambient light filtering in from the curtained windows in the living room just beyond. The backing is a collage of black, rust, and scarlet fabrics.

Primarily cotton, but she splurged on dark red sateen for a lovely liquid texture. The thinnest silver thread she could find is layered atop, creating a web any spider might be proud of. Carefully placed and fashioned with bone-colored embroidery thread are the curving skeletons of small animals: rats, cats, a small dog.

"Wow," hums Clark. "It is ... very unique. So intricate."

"Thank you." Marnie breathes, stroking over one of the spines. "You know, each bone is hand-wrapped. Except for the teeth, of course."

There is quiet. Then Morgan, in his deep voice, "Marnie? Are you saying that these are all real skeletons underneath?"

"This isn't even my best work!" She is excited now. Finally, people to share her work with. Who think she is good enough. She does not even notice as Morgan unclips his walkie from his belt, too focused on ushering the officers—her new friends!—into the living room to meet Mother.

"Oh Jesus," one of them breathes as Marnie's greatest and most reviled piece is revealed.

She once read that many artists hated their masterpieces. So, it only made sense to Marnie to create with the very thing she hated most.

She'd wanted to get it right. She'd borrowed books from the library on taxidermy. And she'd practiced. But it was hard, and she didn't have all the right tools. She'd done her best! And then, of course, she'd needed to do repairs. No matter how careful she'd been, there were still alterations. Fluid gathered, and seams split all the time! She was always gathering materials from all over the neighborhood. Trying to dry the skins in the oven, but most of them burned. And she'd read about using oils in the brain to tan hides. That meant less waste, but it was such a mess! Always a mess.

It was a labor to stitch so carefully along the veins, to trace delicate threads up arms and legs. To embroider the many age spots. To pluck out the brittle, gray, and white hairs on the head and replace them, stabbing the wool into the scalp with the felting needles again and again, the tips breaking on bone. How her fingers had cramped and bled. How her back had ached.

And how carefully she had sewn her mother's mouth shut, coating the threads with her mother's favorite lipstick. It was the least she could do. But it hadn't been enough. Her mother ignored the stitches and the work and kept right on talking, berating, and bemoaning. Marnie couldn't even do that right. Couldn't even silence her properly.

"How dare you, girl? I'm not fit for company!"

"Oh, Mother, please! They just want to see!" But Marnie was nervous now, eyes narrowing in on the small mistakes. The little details. A pulled thread there. A split seam where one of the skins was separating from the main piece. The mismatched eyes, too small by far. She'd use glass next. It wouldn't be the same, but they would last longer.

Mother sits beneath hundreds of unused, scratch-away lotto tickets strung from the ceiling with dozens of colors of thread. They spin lazily between rolls of fly paper like decorations for a macabre gambling party.

She taps a finger to her swollen lip as she fancies art critics do. "What do you think of the chair? Mother says it is tacky and gauche. Is it tacky and gauche?" Marnie had never worked with a glue gun before but liked the effect. Skulls and some of the bigger bones clinging to the old, push wheelchair. The glue had left lovely, thin trails, making the wheels look like webs. Marnie likes it. She thinks it brings the whole piece together. But she never knows what other people will think. Only Mother's opinion.

Turning, she hears Morgan gagging in the hallway, his walkie chirping as a static voice asks him to repeat himself. Clark is just staring, marveling, doe eyes wide.

"You're speechless," Marnie says, nose running, grateful. "You've never seen anything like it before, have you?"

Clark slowly shakes her head, white as the bones Marnie has been bleaching for months now. White as the fresh snow behind the QT when she last collected supplies.

"You see, mother? She's amazed! Aren't you proud of me, Mother? *Mother?*"

SKELETON BIRD SONG
BY M. HALSTEAD

When the first bird emerged, my mother told me, "You're a woman now."

My friends' mothers had said similar things to them, but mine hadn't cared about blood swirling in a toilet. She hardly cared when I spent a whole day kneeling on the linoleum floor and dry heaving into the toilet until she poked her head in at the end of the night and saw the ink-dark feathers floating amongst the bile.

Half-blind, my vision a quilt of night sky and bathroom, at first I didn't understand what was happening. I felt her fingers wrap around my wrist, and I tripped as she hauled me to my feet. I guess I should feel lucky that our bungalow is only one floor because I didn't fall onto the ground until she dragged me down the porch steps. The grit that tore into my knee didn't feel like luck, though.

The feathers and claws dragging their way from my stomach to my throat felt much the same outside as they did on the bathroom tile. I was already sweaty from the effort, and the summer sun beating on my neck just worsened; I got so dizzy I thought I'd pass out. My mother hit me on the back as if I were still a babe with colic, but it didn't help. Every time she did, the

49

bird's beak would hit the skin inside my throat, and more of my blood ended up on the lawn.

There were moments when I couldn't breathe just before the birth. My jaw was wrenched open, my ears popped, my sinuses and brain screamed with pressure. My mother could see the bird and shouted encouragement that I couldn't hear; its head blocked my nostrils, its feet kicked at my larynx. Then, my mother pulled. Her fingers tore at the corners of my mouth as she grasped the bird and yanked, spilling it and the contents of my stomach onto the grass.

"The first one's always the hardest," she assured me as I hacked up the last feathers. "You'll be able to do it on your own soon. Next time, tell me."

I nodded. She didn't comment on my tears or my disheveled body. She took the bird to the aviary and left me there.

I didn't tell her the next time, and it never got easier. Maybe I missed some essential mother-daughter education that makes it easier to grow a bird in your stomach and deliver it through your mouth, and that's why I still struggle. But I didn't ask for the birds, and I resented her for birthing me and grooming me to be her replacement, so I created the birds and killed them.

"Don't worry," she said. "Sometimes there's a long time between your first and your second. It'll come."

It had come, and I had broken its neck and buried it in the woods. I hadn't seen what my first was, but my second was a speckled brown sparrow with a yellow-tinged head—a Henslow's sparrow, I was reasonably certain. It felt smaller than the first but getting it out was a fight every step of the way. I had managed to reach into my throat and pull it out myself, but the pool of blood on the tile was not small.

I couldn't stop thinking about it. It haunted me—the warm brown of its wings, its gently curved beak, its beady eyes. It was fully grown—would that I could create fledglings or eggs!—but seemed to me an infant. There was a sentiment I kept locked deep within my soul about its relation to me. Was it my child? However unwanted, however disgusting I found it, a small corner of my heart couldn't shake that question.

I buried the next in the same area and spent a long time looking at where I had buried the Henslow's. When I covered it with dirt, the forest floor had been alive with wildflowers; now, it lay under a carpet of crackly leaves. I combed them aside and sank my fingers into the cold earth. Autumn numbed them, but when I touched the bones, warmth tickled me. I excavated the tiny skeleton, picked clean by the scavengers in the dirt, and gazed at the tiny wing bones, at the skull, at its fragility. I saw where the neck bones had cracked.

It is under my bed now, in a locked trunk meant to hold my off-season clothes.

As time passed, I buried more of my birds and collected more of their skeletons, and as the clock approached the witching hour, I gazed at the remnants of my unwanted children. Rarely, I told my mother I was about to have one to keep her from being suspicious. She fretted over my health and worried about the frequency, and in my selfishness, I allowed her to think me too ill to carry on the family legacy.

This was my normal in the *before*. Then came the *after*.

I itched to dig her up and add her to my collection. The priest buried my mother in the county cemetery because she hadn't thrown her lot in with either the Methodists or the Baptists, so no minister's wife kept a wary eye on the fretful souls from the parish window. They had trapped her in a coffin, so I knew her skeleton wouldn't be clean if I found it, not the way my birds' bones were. It would be a simple act to clamber over the fence and dig through the soil until I found her, but how could I carry a rotten body home with me? I couldn't put her in my backpack, and anyway, I didn't want maggots or blowflies to nest there. And what would happen when the county realized someone had pilfered my mother's grave? We didn't have grave robbers in Halcomb County. It would cause a stir, and if there's one thing you don't do when your whole *thing* is puking up birds in your backyard, it's causing a stir.

The aviary grew silent. I stopped burying the corpses and just tossed the bodies on the topsoil so they'd decompose faster. I no longer allowed any to live. Eventually, the woods grew silent, too.

"Hi, it's a beautiful day, isn't it!"

The woman on my doorstep was younger than me and hipper, too. I forget, now, what exactly she looked like, but I remember her nails. They were manicured—a far cry from mine, bitten to the quick. They had no color, just white tips, and a glossy overcoat. They weren't obnoxious, but they didn't fit my life. They didn't belong in these hills.

She introduced herself. I don't remember her name or major, but it had something to do with the environment, and she was from Newbank Norton College. "It's so nice out today, isn't it!" she said again.

I agreed that it was.

"But open your ears a little," she said, tapping her own ear with her pen. "What do you hear?"

I told her nothing because it was true; there were the ambient sounds of the area, but I didn't live near anyone to make noise.

"*Bin*-go!" She brandished her pen at me. "You don't hear *anything*! Something is *missing* from what we *ought* to be hearing. When's the last time you heard a bird sing around here?"

We stood in uncomfortable silence for a minute because she was waiting for me to answer, and I did not allow myself to tell her the truth, but still did not want to tell her a lie.

Eventually, she said, "The NNC Ornithological Club is working with the Audubon Society to find out *why* biodiversity has plummeted in the region, and we *believe* local residents may have *valuable* information to help us solve the mystery! Bird populations have sharply declined in the past three years, *especially* in Halcomb County, and we'd like to have a discussion with you and your neighbors about why! We're holding a meeting next Thursday evening in First United Methodist Church's basement—can I mark you down with an RSVP?"

I told her I was very sorry, but I didn't think I'd be able to make it. I shut the door before she could try to convince me again.

She loved it when people did the bird surveys. She'd prowl through the raw data from the college bird club, the Audubon

Society, the state's natural history museum. She kept a little notebook where she'd record percentages, full of hand-made graphs showing the rise or decline of species. She was able to do what I could not: focus her mind to bring forth more of one bird or less of another. Tens of dog-eared ornithological manuals lined the shelf, and she'd calculate where the ecology was falling out of balance.

No matter what she did, the hills never righted themselves. She couldn't understand because birds were the keystone species, and how could maintaining their population not fix everything? She didn't see the mansions being built on cliffs, the swathes of retirees and their sports cars and golf resorts nestling into a place they did not understand. She didn't know about the landfill on the other side of Henfield Knob that was leaking into the waterways. She didn't know what the birds faced when they left the aviary.

Open your ears a little. It's a beautiful day, isn't it? Something is missing. Open your ears. Birds sing. When was the last time you heard a bird sing? When was the last time you let a bird sing? When was the last time you sang? Do the skeletons under your bed sing? Can you sing? Open your ears a little. Maybe then you'll hear the skeleton's song.

When the first bird emerged, my mother told me, "You're a woman, now." She was wrong. If I were a woman at that moment, I would have understood. I would have known to reject that concept of womanhood. I am not a mother, and I am a woman. Women wake up in the morning, and they go to work, and they eat salads and sweets and everything else, and they are kind, and they love their friends and their family, and they are messy, and they are unkind, and they make mistakes, and nowhere does it say that you are not a woman if you do not create life. That's a lie they made up along the way to keep us in line, to hold us down from everything and anything we are meant to be. The birds are a curse my mother passed down to me, even if she didn't see it that way.

When that woman with her perfect nails stood on my doorstep, she could have said anything, but all I heard was *Where are the birds? Why are you killing them?* In the weeks after she left, I rebelled. There is one in my stomach now; I can feel its feathers tickling my insides, and I rebel against it. I squash it down and refuse to let it come out. I don't want the birds anymore. I never did, but this time, I want it to end for good. I don't care if the end result is the bird tearing through my stomach lining and then my fat and then my skin and fluttering away and leaving me to bleed out on the floor.

It will live. That one bird who tears through my stomach will live. It will never know the cost of its life beyond returning to my body to pick the maggots off my skin. It will not know that I had the power to give it a mate, siblings, or keep its entire species from the brink of extinction. It will be entirely on its own. I will be a mother like my mother before me, but in becoming so, I will lay down her load. It was never ours to bear alone.

GRENDELSONG:
A MEREWIF'S LAMENT
BY CARINA BISSETT

It begins with birds,
the early signs omens,
prayers spelled in crayon,
erasable markers,
evil lurking behind stone eyes
painted blue—a warding.

The scene: an accident,
and you too young to know
better than to stomp-crush
a featherless fledgling,
lacy viscera left behind
in the imprint of your shoe.

I knew then, I'd left too late
to flee the curse, the harrowing
rumors of a hag, a hell-bride,
instead of a warrior queen
armed with a kitchen knife
against a murderous man.

I pray it's a mistake,
that you've escaped your fate,
the stain upon your father's brow
and mine, but then I find the others,
nests overturned, contents strewn,
shells shattered, scattered—a litany.

I brew folk remedies, kitchen witch
concoctions of chamomile, lemon balm,
valerian to subdue the rising tide.
You respond with a message, a gift—
a tabby cat's tiger-striped ears
and tattered tail placed upon my pillow.

I offer sacraments, blood-fueled blessings:
ox tails and tongues, liver, and lungs.
When that fails, we return to my lake
where we prowl dark waters, predators
armed with silver spears honed to hunt,
and you emerge, a boy no longer but a man.

For a while, it works, your attention
captured by the beauty, the violence
an underwater dance of teeth and bone,
the scales weighted in your favor
until the day you recognize the distraction
and your gaze returns to the surface

to the sight of pale limbs splashing,
the sound of children's laughter
bright as the day you were born—
and I am defeated, forced to drag you down
to the depths, to death together,
forever, a mother and her monster.

MOTHER, DAEMON, GHOST
BY STEPHANIE M. WYTOVICH

Chloe looked at her naked body and touched the pin to her skin. She dragged it along her clavicle and inched down her side before settling on her navel. Her flesh there was already tender, raw from the last time she cut.

She bit her lip and sucked in a deep breath.

You are strong. You are capable. You are powerful.

Chloe removed the picture of her mother that was jammed into the top corner of her vanity mirror. She had long, wavy brown hair, swamp-green eyes, and a jagged scar on her top lip that always unsettled their neighbors and her childhood friends. Even Chloe could admit it was hard not to look at, but selfishly, it also made her smile, especially when she remembered how it felt to cut her mom for the first time. The look on her face? The abject terror? The blood was darker than she remembered, more than she expected, but still nothing compared to some of their later fights.

Her bedroom light flickered at the memory.

The last time Chloe saw her mother was three years ago. After decades of not speaking, she woke up to a fifteen-minute voicemail of her mother screaming, laughing, breaking glass.

Frantic, she'd called repeatedly, but the phone only rang, Chloe growing more frantic by the second.

What if this is another trick to get me back home? Then again, what if it's not? What if she's finally taken it too far this time? Do I care?

When Chloe was seven, she'd asked her mother if she could spend the weekend at a friend's house. Her mother threw her breakfast against the wall, the wet slap of scrambled eggs a tongue down her neck.

At thirteen, when Chloe had her first boyfriend, her mother found out when he unexpectedly showed up with daisies on the front porch. She'd spat in the boy's face and spent the night howling and praying in her room, the flowers the boy brought left outside to soak in the rain and the cold.

As Chloe got older, she learned to keep her distance, even though distance was the very thing that drove her mother into these manic spells. Terrified at being abandoned, she'd placed locks on Chloe's doors in high school, screwed her windows shut on the full moon. It took everything in her to let Chloe go to school, but the threats from the administrative office kept her grounded enough to let her daughter out for short periods of time. Chloe took to wearing long sleeves to hide the bruises around her wrist, all those little reminders of how hard her mother loved her.

"It's you and me, child," she'd say. "You and me."

The first chance Chloe had to leave, she'd taken it. She'd applied to a college without her mother knowing, used a different address to avoid her intercepting the mail. She'd been saving up money here and there from odd, unsavory jobs she'd do on the internet—always careful to never show her face—and when the acceptance letter came, she'd made plans to leave in the middle of the night. She promised herself she'd never come back home.

That was thirty years ago.

Since then, the attempts at contact came less frequently from her mother, but when they did come, they grew scarier, more intense. Despite never giving her mother her address, on her 25th birthday, she received a box full of dead crows, each with a handwritten letter tied to one of their legs.

I grew your bones.

Your tongue has licked the inside of my womb.

One Valentine's Day in her late thirties, her mother sent her a vial of her blood with a note instructing her to drink it. Chloe moved later that year.

It went on like that for years. Chloe would make friends, would try to date, start new jobs, but something was always there, quietly threatening her. She'd have nightmares of deep holes on snowy nights, holes that grew bigger the longer she looked at them. Sometimes, she'd find herself daydreaming of skinning a deer, her hands red with the touch of its death. She'd taken to washing her hands repeatedly throughout the day, afraid the blood would seep through and appear for everyone else to see.

One time at work, she was making coffee and found maggots in the sugar, their tiny fat bodies wriggling, eager to bury themselves in the wetness of her throat.

She threw up on one of her coworkers, and HR sent her home.

Chloe had grown to expect these little torments, these attempts at guilting her, trying to torture her back home, but the voicemail felt different somehow, desperate, maybe. Chloe worried that if she let this one go, something worse would be waiting for her on the other side.

She got the call from the police a few days later.

Standing barefoot in her childhood home, Chloe couldn't shake the draft that slipped through the cracks in the front door. Everything looked the same as when she'd left, complete with her old winter jacket and her yellow messenger bag shoved into the corner at the bottom of the steps.

Pictures of her and her mother hung on the wall, a thin layer of dust coating forced smiles and stiff shoulders. There were half-drank cups of coffee everywhere she looked. A thin film of mold floated in some of them. Ash and bugs swam in others. Near the closet sat her mother's slippers, tied together with twigs and twine, the soles stapled together to keep them from falling apart.

As Chloe walked through the living room, she couldn't help but touch the couch, the chairs, the TV stand. A soft static hummed in her head. It was hard not to think of all the times she'd torn through this room, tears streaming down her cheeks, a scream tight on her lips. She spotted a soft indent on the stairway wall and rubbed the back of her head where four stitches used to exist.

You really did it this time, didn't you, Mom?

A loose strand of caution tape hung off the archway into the kitchen. From a distance, it looked like it was waving, beckoning her closer. Chloe walked toward it, hypnotized by the tragedy awaiting her, unable to look away, even though the cops warned her in advance.

It was worse than she imagined.

The scent of burning hung thick in the air. The shadows of black candle wax collected on the countertops, kitchen table, and floor tiles. Ash coated the light bulbs and gave a haunted feel to the room, almost like she was looking at it through a piece of fine lace. A mess of flies swarmed the refrigerator while others bumped their bodies against the screen door, anxious to get in.

They can still smell the rot.

The police told her they had also removed a rabbit's body from the scene. It had been covered in honey and dipped in sugar, but thorns were placed through its mouth, eyes, and ears. Four mason jars of blood—animal or human was yet to be determined—were recovered in addition to a knife, a ball of twine, and a travel-sized sewing kit. When she didn't respond, they threw around words like dementia, schizophrenia, and asked her if their family had a history of mental illness. Chloe shook her head no, stifled the desire to tell them there wasn't a name for women like her mother.

And that was after seeing how the woman had sewn her own eyes shut.

Chloe pulled the rusted metal chair out from underneath the table and sat down, her head resting in her hands. When police arrived at the scene, her mother's body had been sitting for three days. She pictured her mother's diminutive frame twice its size, green with the blush of decomp, the smell of sour milk and earth attached to the walls. Her left wrist had been slit, the cut climbing her arm to her elbow, and the crime scene photos had shown some plant smashed into the wound.

Knotweed. That bitch.

Her mother was slumped forward in the chair, a pool of blood at her feet, and before her, Chloe's name was carved into the table and smeared on the walls in what looked to be bile or urine mixed with herbs. The police asked if she knew what this meant, but there was no point.

The damage had already been done.

Chloe pushed the memory out of her head and went to the sink for a glass of water. The forensic cleaners had done a nice job erasing the scene, but the taste of violence still sat in the house. She knew she didn't have a lot of time.

Her mother's favorite mug sat near the faucet, and without giving it a second thought, she filled it full of tap water and greedily gulped it down. Something hard hit her back tooth, and she spat it out, trying not to choke.

In her palm sat a molar, one of her mother's teeth.

Chloe grabbed a chair to steady herself, but the room spun in circles. The hair on the nape of her neck stood on edge, and chills swept down her shoulders and arms. She felt herself begin to sweat.

Come on, come on. Pull yourself together.

She crouched down, put her head between her knees, and closed her eyes. She counted her breaths in the 4-7-8 pattern her therapist had taught her, and when she felt centered enough to open her eyes, she did. That's when she noticed one of the tiles beneath the table. It had a symbol in the lower left-hand corner—an infinity symbol?—barely noticeable, but definitely there.

She ran her finger over it, and nothing budged or loosened, so she took a knife from the carving block and stabbed at the grout until the knife went straight through. There was a hollow space beneath it, and she hacked at the surrounding tiles until she could get a hand underneath to see what her mother was hiding.

It was a box, small but definitely there.

Chloe pulled it out and sat it in her lap, shaking.

Inside was a lock of what she assumed was her hair—kept from a first haircut, perhaps—and it sat next to a jar of fingernail clippings, baby teeth, and dead skin that her mom had peeled off her body one time after a bad sunburn. There was even a pair of underwear covered in light blossoms of blood from her first period. Chloe shuddered in disgust. She knew her mother kept everything of hers, demanded it, in fact, but it was the photographs underneath that bothered her the most. Each one showed the two of them together, and her mother had scratched a crude smile over Chloe's young face and drawn thin dark lines over her own eyes. Each individual photograph was wrapped in twine and red thread.

"A binding," Chloe said, dropping the box. "Fuck."

She collected her things and immediately left the house.

Three years had passed since she stood in her mother's kitchen. She'd sold the house, changed her last name, and upped her medication, but every time she went to sleep, she saw her mother flying above her, arms outstretched, mouth open, the taste of burial lodged in her mouth.

When Chloe caved and switched apartments, her sleep paralysis only got worse, and over the past few weeks, her mother had gotten closer and closer to her body. Some nights, her mother's hair would creep into her mouth. Other nights, the tips of their noses almost touched. Chloe would wake up shaken and soaked in sweat, her eyes bloodshot and tired.

She'd met with psychics, visited priests, and tried everything from floor washes to taking twice-daily salt baths to doing egg cleanses in the evening. Still, there were continued footprints on her floor, her skin broke out in rashes, and the eggs broke bloody into glasses, some with floating eyes. One even contained a beak.

Her anxiety kept her home most days now, which was ironic because home was the last place she'd wanted to be, but when she went outside, she'd see visions of headless dogs, watch people's faces blur as they walked past her. One time, while driving to work, she saw her mother hanging from the stoplight, her neck broken, a wide smile on her face. And after rear-ending the car in front of her, she quit her job and looked for something remote.

"There's no such thing as ghosts," her friends would say, but Chloe had been haunted by this woman in life, and she knew death wasn't going to put an end to her ways.

That's when she started writing to her mom.

Every morning, she'd get up just before dawn and handwrite a letter begging her to leave. She'd sign it with her original name and punch a hole on both sides of the paper. Then, she'd weave a piece of twine through each end and tie them both to a black candle, one with her name carved into it, the other with her mother's. After that, she'd wait for the first rays of sun to peak over the hill, and then she'd light the candle and sit there while it burned.

It was a classic unbinding spell, one of the few pieces of magic she'd learned as a child, but the only thing it accomplished was a week of temporary blindness and an afternoon of shattering mirrors and crickets in her bathroom sink.

Maybe the spell alone isn't strong enough.

Chloe paced her bedroom and went through the resource library in her head.

Poisonous plants. Hexes. Sour jars. Grounding rituals.

Her anxiety had gotten so bad that the strain from grinding her teeth often locked her jaw, and she worried if she wrung her hands any more, they'd likely reshape into claws.

She picked up her phone and went through her saved voicemails. She played her mother's screams on repeat, listening to the wildness in her voice. After the fifth or sixth time, she ran to the bathroom and threw up. Bile splashed violently against the toilet's rim as tears spilled down her face. Her body couldn't handle this constant state of fear and torture.

After a minute or two of dry heaves and no liquid, she opened her eyes and saw a piece of red thread swimming in the bowl.

She stared at it for a few minutes before she wiped her mouth and threw open the bathroom cabinet. She pushed away the extra bottles of shampoo and mouthwash she'd hoarded with coupons until, in the back corner, underneath a basket of hair ties and scrunchies, she found what she was looking for: the wooden box.

The same wooden box she'd found underneath the tile in her mother's kitchen.

Chloe opened it and stared at the pictures, at the pieces of her crammed into jars. Rage consumed her.

She didn't know why she'd kept it, but she knew she couldn't just throw it away either. So, for years, it had hidden in the shadows like a dark secret, something she'd tried hard to forget.

But no more.

Chloe picked up the box and went into her room to pack a bag.

Two can play at this game, Mom.

Chloe drove what was now an eleven-hour drive back to her hometown and turned into St. Lucia's Cemetery. Rain beat against the windshield, and even with the wipers on full blast, she could hardly see more than a few feet in front of her.

She pulled off the side of the road and turned off her lights. She hadn't attended her mother's burial, and while she didn't feel guilt over that decision, the thought of an empty service with a lone man saying prayers suddenly filled her with a sense of grief.

Part of her wondered if anyone had ever visited her mother's grave, but the other half knew.

Chloe exited the car, grabbed her bag, and turned on her flashlight. Skeletal trees reached toward a dark sky while the crisp fall air beat against her face in sharp gusts of wind. She'd looked up the gravesite beforehand, but now that she was here, the adrenaline high that pushed her straight through the drive had started to wear off. After all, there wouldn't be any undoing what she was about to do, and she hated the thought that this act could somehow bind them further, making things worse.

The whole thing seemed insane, a death wish.

But that's why she needed to do it.

Like mother, like daughter.

It was worth the risk.

Chloe found her mother's grave at the bottom of a hill, tucked away near the edge of the trees. There was a simple stone pushed into the ground that read *Josephina Gilbert, 1952-2018*. There weren't any flowers or statues, but black feathers littered the ground, and dead spiders collected near her name.

She took the candles out of the bag and set them near the stone next to a picture of her mom. She made a thick circle of salt around her, careful to avoid any openings. If anyone saw her, it would just look like she was praying, which she supposed, in some manner, she was. It wasn't until she took out the nails, the knife, some Yerba Santa, and the wooden box now lined with mirrors that the tone of the evening changed.

The night sky seemed to grow darker as she pushed the nails through the salt and into the ground. Chloe lit a match and held it against the herbs.

"I invoke you, Josephina Gilbert. Mother, demon, ghost. I call you on your grave, invite you to seek solace in my flesh." She waved the smoke around the grave in sweeping, lush movements. She repeated the incantation two more times and then added, "I seal my apology in blood."

Chloe set the still-smoking herbs on the grave and picked up the knife. She pulled her shirt over her head and felt a chill sweep across her chest. Her body shone pale against the starless sky as she took a deep breath, a tear stealing down her cheek.

The knife cut easily, her blood eager to flow. It ran down her palm faster than she'd expected, and she hurriedly pressed it into the dirt, scraping at the earth with her hands. *Waste not.* After she'd collected enough loose soil, she scooped it up and brought it to her mouth. She only hesitated for a moment before she swallowed it greedily, the taste of funerals and earthworms dancing on her tongue.

She repeated like two more times.

As above, so below, as within.

In between fits of gagging, some forced, others involuntary, she began to carve. Blood seeped down her shoulders, her breasts, and her waist as she repeatedly wrote her mother's name across her body. She shook and cried, the pain immaculate, but she needed to get her mother's attention. The woman needed to know she was serious.

"Josephina!" she screamed. "Mother … Mother, I'm so sorry." Chloe outstretched her arms, her head swimming and dizzy from blood loss. "Forgive me. I should have been there."

The trees seemed to smile as they waved their arthritic limbs in her direction. The ground exhaled, releasing a long, sought-out breath. Chloe opened blurry eyes to see her mother's visage, a slumped shadow kneeling in the distance, statuesque and just out of reach.

An owl screeched in the distance.

A car alarm went off.

Josephina tilted her head, and her arms fell behind her back, her torso bending into a bridge. She scuttled toward her daughter, her movements like snapped twigs, broken bones.

She stopped outside the circle, her eyes locked on the grave as she reassembled her body. A beetle pushed through her mother's mouth and reburied itself in her right eye.

Chloe extended her hand, blood dripping from her fingertips.

Come on, take the bait …

Josephina studied the girl in an unbroken stare before bringing the girl's fingers to her mouth. She licked at them first, a sample, an aperitif, before her jaw unhinged, her mouth a gaping hole of spiderwebs and dust. She clamped down on Chloe's hand, salvia dripping down the girl's wrist. A smile broke across Josephina's dirt-stained lips as she closed her eyes and lost herself in lust.

In that short moment of disconnect, Chloe opened the box behind her with her other hand. She softly picked it up and placed it in her lap, the tightening of her muscles a silent alarm.

Her mother opened her snake-like eyes and howled at her reflection in the mirrors, unable to look away.

"I sever you, Mother, I cut the cord. You are bound, linked to no one ... but ... yourself," Chloe said, her breath wavering from the blood loss. "I collect you, entrap you, shed my blood for yours."

Chloe collapsed then, her wounds pressed to and soaking the earth. Desperate for warmth, she reached for one of the feathers near the grave and savored its softness.

Please, please ...

The scenery blinked in and out of focus, her mother's screams barbaric and inhumane. The nails Chloe had placed in the ground leaped from their positions and flew toward her mother, pinning her spirit in place. The mirrors glowed hot as the woman's reflection danced within them, naked and burning, her essence disappearing in violent strips and hacks.

Before Chloe closed her eyes, she saw her mother's tongue, long and forked, reach out toward her for one final taste.

When she woke up, it was morning, and the walls around her were white.

"Miss Gilbert, can you walk me through what happened that night in the cemetery?" the doctor asked. A notepad sat in his lap, and she could smell his coffee from across the room. Black, stale. He'd probably warmed it up twice already.

"I'd rather not talk about it," Chloe said. She picked at the skin around her thumb, pulling it back and ripping it off until she bled. She'd been at the hospital for three days now. Psychiatric observation for the cuts on her body.

"You know the rules," he said. "I can't sign off on your release until I know you're not a threat to yourself."

"And you know that I won't say a damn word until you tell me where the box is," Chloe said, her voice sharp, a quick stab.

They'd been through this twice already. When she initially woke up, there were hands all over her and an oxygen mask on her face. Her upper body was wrapped in gauze, and the smell of antiseptic stood strong in the room. She screamed and thrashed against them, an anxious, haunted thing. She had no memory of how things ended: the circle, her mother. What had happened to the nails?

"The box is safe," he said. "Along with the rest of your possessions that came in with you. You'll get them back when we deem you're no longer a threat to yourself or those around you."

I was never the threat . . .

"Fine. I was paying my respects to my mother," Chloe said.

The doctor nodded, pleased she'd given something up. "Yes, I'm sorry to hear of her passing. Were the two of you close?" he asked.

Chloe laughed. "I guess you could say that."

His office was relatively small, much smaller than she would have imagined for someone in his position. She sat on an uncomfortable mass-produced couch the color of a rotting orange and scanned the room. Bookshelves lined the walls and were draped in a soft light that she much preferred to the bright fluorescents outside. There was a basket of fidget toys underneath the end table to her left and a row of succulents sunned themselves on the window ledge.

She hoped the cold killed them.

The doctor wrote something down on his notepad. "Okay. Can you describe your relationship to her?"

Painful. Terrifying. Heartbreaking. Traumatic.

"It was complicated," Chloe said. "We fell out of touch for some time." She continued to pick at her thumb, the blood darker now, starting to drip down her hand.

"Because you're an ungrateful bitch?"

Chloe almost fell out of her chair. "Excuse me?"

"I said, because you're an ungrateful bitch," the doctor repeated, his tone unphased by the rise in her voice.

Speechless, Chloe sat there, unable to move. "I don't think—"

"Yes, you strike me as someone who *doesn't* think. Just acts, right? Acts without any concern to who they're ignoring, hurting, cutting, trapping …"

Trapping?

Before she could move, he was between her legs, her wrist in his hand, his tongue flicking toward her, begging, teasing at the blood.

Chloe screamed, but the doctor just laughed, a threatening grin creeping up the side of his face. He clawed at his chest, his skin falling off in large, bloody clumps. He pulled his hair, extending it far down his back. Shocked, Chloe watched as he slapped at his face, his nose breaking, his eyes turning green.

A crow slammed against the window.

Then another.

And another.

The man stood up and began jumping, his feet violent against the floor. Every time he landed, the room shook. Books fell off the walls. Folders slid from his desk.

Chloe watched as feathers collected in her lap, as roots broke through the tiled floor and reached for her legs.

No. No. No.

The room shattered, a broken mirror, a cracked wall.

In its place was the dirt, the cemetery, the nightmare; her body still slit and bleeding, cold and alone near the grave. A faint tendril of smoke curled in the air, and beside her sat the box, her mother nowhere to be found.

Chloe thought about reaching for her phone but couldn't feel her arms.

She didn't need help, though. This part, she could do on her own.

Memories of missed opportunities and guilt trips played through her head. The time she didn't wash the dishes, so her mother didn't feed her for two days. The missed dances, the ruined birthdays. The time her ninth-grade teacher asked her why she kept falling asleep in class.

Her mother had been preparing her for this moment for years, teaching her how to slip into walls, sink into floorboards, speak in whispers, dress in echoes.

All she had to do now was wait.

Wait for the bloodletting, wait for the erasure, wait for what mother taught her how to do best.

To disappear and fade.

Finally, become the ghost that Mother had always wanted.

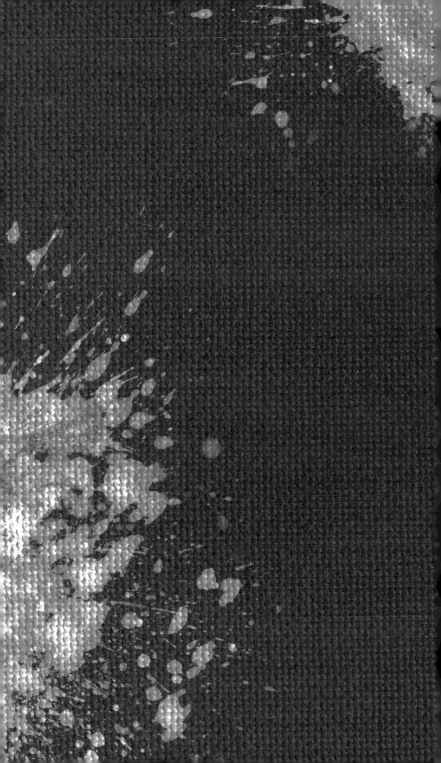

MOUTHPIECE
BY CAROL EDWARDS

The demon has her place.
She does not wait for me to wake to start her screaming.
She comes to find me, scratching at walls
pulling door handles
dripping her acid into my ears.
It eats through the sleeping window, seeps along shadowed paths
that pulse rhythms to the spirits in my body.
They cannot help but commune in electric sparks.

The demon sets fire to roots squirming deep in gray soil
feeding dark beats from a taut drum.
Truth re-invents itself again, whispers stories to the flowers

struggling to rise. They curl in on themselves
green skin cellophaned to tender bones
mummies with burnt faces; each one I could snap off.

The demon lurks in her place, quiet in the dawn hour.
Her hungry shrieks have consumed windows and drums and
flowers.
I lie wheat-golden, my limbs full of searing light
lungs made of hissing leaves
heart shedding seeds that will never eat the sun –
all mouths speak in unison.

COOKIE BABY
BY LAURA CRANEHILL

The baby is gone now, but Maddy knows how to make Mom happy again.

Maddy kneads the dough. Sprinkles the molasses flesh with powdered sugar. Twists the tummy like the knot of a pretzel. Dollops of frosted cream, buttons of jelly, a meringue smile.

Her hands floury and fluffy as new-fallen snow, *pat pat pat*, Maddy brings new life where there was none. Breath where there was wind, skin where there was sugar, heartbeat where there was only heart shape. The ginger girl's bulge of lips gasp open, like a tiny oven swinging agape, and hot honey breath so sugar sweet pours from her brown tongue. When Maddy leans in to give a kiss, it is a kiss of caramelized cinnamon fragrance. Maddy has made something good, something holy.

Maddy walks whisper-soft on bunny slippers, still flushed with the joy of creation, and creeps gently to the armchair where Mom sleeps. She lays the tray next to Mom's silk, pearl-dotted slippers.

Maddy doesn't want to miss when Mom wakes, doesn't want to miss the smile that will come to Mom's naked lips. Mom hasn't worn lipstick, ChapStick, or a smile since the baby. Maddy falls asleep, waiting.

When she startles awake from a bad dream, she sees the last of the cookie's blue-button eyes disappear into Mom's chapped maw.

The cookie baby is gone now, but Maddy knows what she did wrong. She made the baby too pretty, too sweet. Most of all, she gave the baby to her mom too early. Right off the tray, still warm, how was her mom to know that the baby wasn't anything but an ordinary cookie?

So, this time, she makes the baby without frosting, without chocolate chips or caramel chews. Just a bare thing, nude and wonderful in its glory.

She lets the baby cool and does not yet show Mom. She lets the baked limbs unfurl naturally, stretch, become self-mobile.

The first thing the baby does is hug Maddy. It's nice and mouse-comfortable, even if the baby's breath is sucralose-bland.

Maddy has a wonderful time playing with her baby sister.

But when Mom finds them in the living room, drawing quietly, she swoops out of the hallway, at first on two legs, then loping on all fours. She comes to the sisters and slides to a crouch. She reaches for Maddy's baby sister.

"Mama, no!" cries Maddy.

Mom's cool, black eyes slide over to Maddy. There's a lesson splayed raw right on the hot meat of Mom's face, the lesson that says some things were never meant to be made, and some things were not meant to be loved, and Maddy better know now, better figure it out now.

Mom's sickle eyes reap, then close. Her eel-dark mouth cracks open, and she gobbles up Maddy's nude baby sister while

Maddy sits and watches Mom eat the thing she loves and learns her lesson.

This time, when Maddy makes a baby, she does not finish it in the kitchen. She huddles in the fireplace at the end of the house and fills the lump of dough with ash. This baby won't be tasty at all! Even if Mom takes a bite, she'll spit the baby out. The baby might have to live the rest of its life missing a chunk, but it will live.

Maddy drags her fingers along the torso and makes little gutters. Rib bones, for hunger. A child who will not expect much.

Maddy goes to the fire and puts the baby in. She hears a noise behind her and hastily takes the baby out, a little singed, a little uncooked. When she turns around, she's relieved to see just a mouse twitching its inquisitive nose.

Even though the dough is baked halfway, Maddy again makes life where before there was nothing.

Right away this time, Maddy realizes her mistake. With all that ash in its flesh, the baby is gray-blue, like the boy, the unbreathing boy, that Mom made.

Immediately, the ash baby is a funny baby. She toddles a bit. Then she pirouettes, she arabesques, she pliés. She toddles again and falls.

Maddy laughs. Her laugh is a strange, foreign presence, tolling through the house like the largest church bell locked in a yawning tower, announcing morning, or another mourning, it's too early to be certain. Maddy's body becomes rigid, afraid suddenly at her own laughing. Afraid she will wake Mom too early, that Mom will emerge from her cavernous bedroom with the perpetually drawn curtain. She will spill out into the hallway, a sea of rage, ready to take revenge on the child whose laughter brought her out of her stupor.

Maddy's heart beats hard and wet, three times, four times, five times until Maddy releases her held breath.

Mom does not wake.

Maddy scoops her new baby sister into her arms and takes her out into the yard, just in case.

Maddy makes a nest for her sister in the hedgerow, a pocket of leaves, dirt, and musty pine needles. Maddy's sister sleeps hidden for a few days, weeks, months even, and grows.

And with her, Maddy's heart grows. This baby brings life to her, too.

One afternoon, Maddy comes in ruddy-cheeked from playing with her little sister and walks down the hallway. She's startled by Mom, standing in that black, empty space between two rooms, still and silent in the dark. Mom reaches out and snatches Maddy's wrist, and Maddy realizes there's a light dust of dough on her fingers. Mom puts Maddy's fingers to the swirl of her crusty mouth and licks.

Don't worry, Maddy tells her pounding heart. *It will just taste like ash, and I will get in trouble for playing in the fireplace again and nothing more.*

But Mom's eyes widen. The amorphous black puddles tighten and click and sharpen to those of a predator.

She searches the house, raging, tearing it apart, yelling her monstrosities, *where is she? Where is she? I will find her, and you will learn your lesson—*

What can Maddy do? We are fragile creatures, all of us, but especially those of us made of dough. Maddy has a choice to make. On one hand, Mom, and on the other, her sister.

Because, you see, like most little girls, Maddy wasn't born with a third hand, where she can choose herself.

Maddy plays games with her sister. She has been playing them for a long time. Games of chase and capture, of winning and losing, of conquering and defeat, of swords, and guns, and long, poisoned needles. Maddy is teaching her little sister to fight.

Maddy looks at the bleak and silent house and wonders if, accidentally, she's been making a choice all along.

Her heart beats hard and long. She doesn't want anyone to get hurt.

And then, one day, they stop their games to watch a butterfly in a cocoon split open its papery outer body and push out, goopy and changed, crawling into the sun to warm itself. And that's when Maddy realizes Mom, too, could be born anew.

Maddy will not have to make any hard choices if Mom changes.

Daddy's at work, and Mom is napping when the two sisters dig out the matches from the loose-change drawer.

Maddy is giddy with excitement. What strange things will happen! To make life ignite in a body already inhabited.

How wonderful it will be. What a bright, brand-new thing her mom will become.

First, the house's insides smolder and burn. Maddy can see flames lick up the windows, then engulf them.

Maddy's little sister, who is just learning to talk, says, "We must bar the door so Mother doesn't come out too early." She blinks down at herself; must be thinking of her own half-cooked flesh.

Maddy is surprised by this full sentence, but she sees the wisdom in it. She smiles and nods, and the two girls bar the door with bikes, toys, branches, and things they find in the yard.

Maddy stands on the sidewalk, breathless, as the house becomes a life-giving oven. One hand on her heart, one holding her little sister's ashy hand, waiting for Mom to come out of the burning house. She's so excited to see what new thing Mom will become.

Mom eventually emerges from the flames, and Maddy barely recognizes her. Her little sister's eyes are wide with wonder and surprise.

Mom is a tiny thing now. Her peripheral parts are gone. The sharp glass edges of her have smoothed and rounded until only the doughy center of her remains. She is a tender, tasty cookie baby.

Mom stumbles, blinking with newborn sight. When she sees Maddy on the sidewalk, she squeals and reaches out. Maddy gathers her up in her arms, and Mom is now so small that she folds gently into Maddy's chest. Maddy's heart pulls and squeezes with love and triumph. Mom's pastry skin is still gooey-sweet, her hot marshmallow breath on Maddy's face. Maddy coos to her gently. Mom coos back.

THERE'S NO PLACE LIKE HOME
BY ROXIE VORHEES

There's no place like home
Unless home is here
Then home is no place

Click your heels three times
Close your eyes, say the words
And when the dream fog lifts
Four barren walls painted nicotine yellow
Are what's behind the curtain.

If only she had a heart
If only I had a brain

Follow the cracked atrous pavement
Around in circles and straight out of town
To the absent matriarch stuck on herself
And the patriarch hiding in his den
Where the stannum shell of a human stands

Do you know the place
Where the reddest apples grow?

Can you see the house,
And could it fall on the witch, please?

Home isn't lined by poppy fields
Or the flying monkey's roost
But a delusion that floats around in a bubble

You can't dress it up in ruby slippers
Or hide it behind emerald lenses
But the wicked witch always dies in the end
Figuratively, not literally

For home is not a place at all
It is safe and quiet and filled with those you love
Home is where you say it is

Have I had it in me all along?

THE HOUSE MOTHER
BY KRISTI DEMEESTER

Marion took the House Mother job the day before her twenty-fifth birthday. Not an old maid by any stretch of the imagination, but with her oatmeal-colored cardigan and sensible shoes, the honey blondes who traipsed in and out of Zeta Tau saw her as something worthy of blending in with the wallpaper. A warning of a future that would never belong to them. They were too pretty, too charming for anything less than a two-carat solitaire by the time the tulips poked their heads through the melting snow their senior year.

Of course, she'd lied on her résumé and during the interview. Marion would be the youngest House Mother by far. Most of them were soft-bodied blue hairs with wrinkled hands and rosy cheeks who doted on their girls like grandmothers. Ran their houses with military precision while keeping the oven filled with cookies their girls would only nibble at. Marion had told the board she was thirty-five. Solidly committed to her life without a husband. Without children.

"Probably barren," one of them had whispered as Marion gathered her things to go. She pretended she hadn't heard as she tugged her cardigan from the back of the chair.

In the end, the extra ten years hadn't mattered. No one remembered her. No one ever remembered her. The board hadn't checked her references or asked for transcripts or proof of her degree, and she moved into the old Greek revival on campus on a Thursday morning.

"We'll do a formal introduction on Sunday during the chapter meeting. Do you have anything white?" Marion opened her mouth, but the board president waved a hand at the words she was still trying to cough up. "Doesn't matter. You'll have time to find something if you don't. Chapter rules. You might not be a sister, but it does a world of good to show solidarity. Reinforce the tenets of sisterhood." She pressed a set of keys into Marion's hand. "Front door, side delivery door, shed, your suite, and then two more that are to God knows what." She dusted her hands together. "Well, that should do it. I trust you can take it from here?"

Marion nodded at the president's retreating back, her hand locked around the keys.

The house was silent as she let herself inside. Morning classes were already in full swing, and those lucky enough to avoid the eight a.m. rush slept on. Marion opened her mouth. Breathed deep. Love Spell body spray. Flat iron singed hair. A fermented, unwashed sourness beneath it all. Girl smells. Private, secret smells. She poked her tongue out to taste. Let her eyes slip closed as she imagined the dust invading her lungs and settling, spore-like, into the meat of her. It was the closest she could get to a possession, and she wondered what sort of incantation would hold such a phantom inside her. Keep it there so it became more of her than the woman she'd become.

The foyer was all marble and gold light fixtures that opened into a large dining area, a gleaming, stainless-steel kitchen on the left, and then another hallway that led to a common area dominated by an oversized leather couch and a television that had no right being as large as it was. Floor-to-ceiling windows poured golden light over the gleaming floors, and a claw-footed table held framed photos of the somber-faced founding sisters. An ornate gold, full-length mirror was propped in the corner, and she avoided looking into it. Didn't want to see herself in this sacred space. It was like stepping into a doll's house. Everything looming over her. Threatening to gobble her up.

At the back, a set of stairs curved up to the bedrooms, the single hallway stretching the entire length of the house. Marion went from door to door, touching the knobs, feeling for any warmth that might linger there, waiting to see if anyone would open their door and scream, a hand pressed to their chest because she'd scared them, but then how they'd laugh and laugh, and she would introduce herself, and the girl would clutch at her hands and tell her how *relieved*, how *happy* she was that Marion was finally home. They'd been waiting for her, and could she show Marion around? They could have lunch together after, and by then, most of the other sisters would be back from class, and they could all get to know each other. So *fun*, right?

She turned one of the handles, felt it give under her touch. Unlocked. All those doors unlocked and waiting for her to finally arrive. But no. She let go of the handle and stepped back. There would be no reason for locked doors in her house. Her girls would leave them open. An invitation and reminder that she was welcome. Wanted, even.

She made her way back down the stairs and through the foyer with its framed composites dating back to the times of big hair and frosted shadow. She paused only to look at the most recent. Told herself she would not look at the composite for spring 2003. The year she'd been a freshman and full of hope her mother would have laughed at if cancer hadn't dissolved her insides.

When she passed the photo without even a glance, Marion gave herself a little pat on the back. She'd have it taken down. Maybe even thrown out. She doubted anyone would notice. And even if they did, she could make something up. Cracked glass. Chipped frame. Easy-peasy.

Another, shorter hallway opened to a study area with a handful of computers, bookshelves crammed with textbooks the bookstore wouldn't buy back even though they were brand new at the start of the semester and three hundred dollars. Red plastic cups covered whatever open surface remained, and two open pizza boxes revealed half-eaten slices of supreme veggie. She frowned and made a mental note to identify which of her girls had befouled her house in such a way.

A shared bathroom, two storage closets, and then the final door. The House Mother's suite. Someone had already placed a placard with her name beside the door. She touched it with careful fingers. Traced the gold script of the name no one recognized. Marion Wallace. Seven years ago, she'd written that same name in pink glitter gel on a name tag, a diamond secreted in a corner so that anyone who saw it would know exactly where she wanted to be. Who she wanted to be.

And now, the room—*this* room, inside *this* house—was hers.

She unlocked the door, and the air that pushed against her as she stepped inside smelled of powder and lilac. Nothing at all like the girl smells the rest of the house carried like holy relics wrought in Bath and Body Works body spray. She wrinkled her nose and coughed, trying to clear her lungs of old lady. Of the reminders that her body would only continue to age. To wrinkle. To gray. Even as the girls around her never changed. Forever blonde. Forever nineteen and twenty with their fake IDs and Daddy's credit card tucked inside their Coach purses.

There was a hard, wooden chair. A mattress and a frame and a set of sheets folded on top. A metal desk and filing cabinet. A telephone with faded numbers scrawled beside the speed dial keys. A plumber. A food distributor. A handyman. Someone known only as Bryan H. She imagined them in the house— their coarse, greased hands touching all those pristine things. Invading the house. *Her* house. Marking it with their scents. She pulled the plug from the wall hard enough for the tiny plastic tab that held it there to snap. She could have crawled inside that sound and eaten it from the inside out.

She slipped off her cardigan. Her blouse and bra. Tugged her skirt and underwear over her hips and let them pool on the floor before spreading herself over the bare mattress. Panted as she breathed in the remaining dust of the previous House Mother—her fingers hooked at the mattress's edge, her hips pushing down and down and down, her mouth and teeth opening as she screamed without sound.

Marion found the hole in the wall three months later. By then, she'd fallen into a routine. Food order for the week on Mondays. Organic and lean proteins. Fruits that her girls giggled over and called "exotic." Housekeeping on Tuesdays with her observing as a team descended on the house and left it smelling of bleach. Landscaping on Thursdays and then family meal, where she sat among them, quiet as she watched them eat the dinners she'd prepared, the pieces of herself she'd secreted inside. Her fingernails. Her saliva. Her monthly blood.

They called her an angel. Blew her kisses. Wrapped their arms around her and said they didn't know how they had lived without her. And each time, it was ecstasy. To be so seen. So wanted.

The weekends were quiet affairs. She kept herself locked in her room, back pressed to the mattress so she would not have to see her girls stumble home, hair limp with bar sweat, and reeking of a stolen, "only when I drink" cigarette. Even less did she want to see the fraternity boys they sneaked in after mixers, all of them the same variant of floppy hair and pastel button-downs and loafers without socks.

On the hungover Sunday mornings, she made them light breakfasts that would go down easy. Coffee. Gatorade. And in the afternoons, she emptied their trashcans that held their used condoms and mounds of tissue and then went into her own private bathroom to vomit and sob and wonder what more she could possibly do to make them see.

They didn't need anything else. Only this house. Only her.

And so, it was a Sunday night when she found the hole. Sunday nights were Chapter nights, and she'd not yet been invited, so Marion used the time to float from room to room. To touch the cool silk of their dresses and open drawers to peek inside at the underwear and push-up bras. All lace and pink. The color of something's wet insides. And she would shiver, knowing they were just downstairs. That any one of them could come upstairs and find her there.

She could feed them an excuse. She was the House Mother, after all, but there would be suspicion. Talk. And she would not be able to bear it. To hear her name whispered from their glossed mouths, their eyes looking everywhere but at her even as she went among them. Like that day seven years ago when she'd come to the house after rush ended. After she'd written only Zeta Tau on pref night even though she'd been told not to. That it was suicide to select only one sorority. And then on Bid Day, when the sisters in that 2003 composite had stared at her with wide eyes and whispered that they'd not given her a bid, so why had she come? She'd stayed until it felt as if her skin had come loose from her bones and then fled back to the dorm, where she sat in the dark, quivering in front of the mirror, watching as the shadows bent her face into something unrecognizable.

Here, in the closet, was a dim rendering of what had come before. A ghost set loose in the rooms where she'd not been invited.

The hole was at the back of the storage closet in the common area. She'd gone hunting for spare towels; thought she remembered seeing a stack of them folded haphazardly on the top shelf.

The closet was deep. The air thick with the dust of previous lives. Shelves with canned peaches that would go uneaten. Boxes filled with cleaning supplies deemed ineffective but never thrown out. The towels weren't on the shelves, and she knelt, pushing aside the boxes as she peered into the dark. Crept forward until the closet swallowed her up, the door swinging closed on silent hinges as she reached a grasping hand forward into that unending black.

She heard them at first. A quiet murmuring that prickled her skin. And then the light—a dim flickering that hinted at candlelight. At ritual.

She pushed forward, her ribs scraping along the floor until she could see into the hole. It was the length and width of her arm. Enough room to place her neck along the jagged strip of drywall and imagine a blade suspended above her. She let the feeling shiver through her, her lips open and panting in anticipation before she looked upward, the phantom of anticipation vanishing as she took in the blank space between the walls. A pinprick of a hole that was the source of the light.

The open space ran along the length of the back of the house, enough room to stand. To walk. To go hidden within the guts of the house, creeping from room to room without being seen.

The drywall crumbled in her hands as she pulled at it, ripped her way into this other, secret world, and then pushed through, the dust covering like a caul. Marked. Holy.

They were singing now. Her girls. Their voices so lovely as they floated through the notes, and she placed her hand against the wall. Felt how it trembled for them. This house. Her own heart.

Their heat pulled her to that secret room. The room she had not known existed with its secret, hidden door. She wondered which of her girls had the key. If she wore it around her neck like a talisman. If it burned her, the scar hidden beneath a pale indentation on her skin, a ribbon her husband's fingers would one day trace as he asked her, jokingly, if it was what kept her head on her neck.

She could hear them behind the wall, and she held herself still. If she'd had a knife, she would have cut herself just to quiet her heart. The heavy rush of her blood drowned out their voices, and she wished for anything that would lessen herself in the face of this unknowable leviathan.

She stayed there, the dark holding her in its great mouth, until she heard chairs shuffling, and then she went tumbling out of the closet, blinking against the sudden, awful light. Brushing the dust from her clothing and hair, she rushed back to the kitchen, where she would finish preparing for the start of the week. They called to her as they passed, wishing her a good night, and she kept her body angled away so they wouldn't see her clothes. The smeared, white dust on her blouse. Her skirt.

She stayed in the kitchen as the house drifted into its nocturnal quiet. Waited until she was the only thing left awake. Like those years when she was a girl. Cold under her thin sheet as she listened for the sound of her mother's car, her stomach clenching around the dinner she'd not eaten because the refrigerator held only mustard and molded cheese and soy sauce packets, even though she should be *grateful* for the roof over their head. The clothes on her back. For the fact that her mother even had a job and was able to provide for them after her father had left to live in sin with his new whore.

As if in remembrance, her stomach ached to be filled, and she licked at the dust on her skin. Took the house into herself as if in holy Communion. Her skin swollen with it. Her stomach filled. She would eat of their body. Their blood. And she would be blessed as they had been.

She found a screwdriver. Went back to the closet and pushed herself inside, the air humid and close as she bore a hole into the wall. A tiny thing. Just enough for her to see that secret room with its long table. Its chairs. The pale oak paneling and the carved crest affixed to the far wall. If she held her nose to the hole, she could still smell them. Her girls. How she'd anointed them with her own scent.

Like any mother, she would know them anywhere.

It felt sacred, on this holiest of days, that her dress was white. She'd gone out earlier in the week and bought it, her hands trembling as she watched the woman behind the register wrap it in tissue paper before placing it reverently in the bag. It was a plain organza, scoop-necked with puffed sleeves. The sort of dress her mother had never allowed her to wear. Why did a little girl need that sort of attention? Pride was a sin, after all. No daughter of hers would go around with her chest on display like some whore.

As she stood before the closet door, she wished for a veil. Not bridal, but a first Communion. A symbol of reverence toward what she was about to witness. What she was about to enact.

It had been Jesus who chose the cross. Who had called out to his father and asked why he had been forsaken, only to be answered in blood. So many times, Marion had chosen righteousness and suffered a crucifixion. She could choose again. Inside the house, there would be a resurrection. And her girls, her precious girls, would bear witness.

She'd not joined them at dinner. Had lain out their repast and gone to her suite, where she scrubbed at her skin until it was raw and pink. Tied her hair back into a simple knot. A sweep of mascara and pink gloss. All the things she'd denied herself since that day when she'd opened up her bid card only to discover Zeta Tau had not offered her a place among them. She'd not been worthy of such vanities. Her mother would have called it a sin. The mascara. The gloss. Would have held her face underwater until she was washed clean. A necessary baptism.

She bared her teeth to the mirror. Wondered if she peeled her skin away, if her bones would be as white. As sharp.

It was silent when she emerged from her suite. She'd locked all the doors earlier that afternoon. Had thrown the keys out the window of her suite before her girls had gone to get ready for Chapter, their heels clicking as they hurried across the foyer.

The closet opened before her like an altar, and as she crossed the threshold, she almost sobbed. Finally, she was home.

The drywall saw was where she'd left it on the highest shelf. Her only other purchase that week, she'd bought it for the feel of the wooden handle in her palm. How it felt almost like holding nothing at all. But she didn't need it. She'd already cut a hole wide enough to fit her body. Taped the drywall back in place with duct tape, knowing no one would notice the seam. Her girls didn't have the capacity for such things. It was why they needed her.

She knew the shape of their meetings now. The lights dimmed as each sister paused to light one of the candles at the front of the room. A call to order and recitation of the motto. The requisite taking of attendance. The treasurer giving her report before the rest of the leadership team's announcements. Open floor for any sister to present any known issues. The president's closing reminders. And then they would sing. Quietly. Each note delicate and airy, and it didn't matter that Marion had heard it six times over; she wept every time. They were so beautiful. Her girls. Her house.

It had been a mistake to rush those seven years ago. It was better for her to come to them this way. As their mother rather than their sister.

The tape came away easily. A little push and then the hole opened, and she almost giggled as she stepped through because none of her girls had heard anything at all. None of them turned to look and see as she crept behind them on all fours. As she knelt just behind them, the drywall saw somehow in her hand even though she hadn't needed it at all.

Her nostrils flared with their scent, and she panted, their salt on her tongue as she reached to touch them. Her girls. That shining, golden hair. So much like the candlelight that cast twisted shadows on the walls.

"My darlings," she whispered. "I'm here now." She wrapped her fingers through that thick hair and tugged. Pressed her teeth against a delicate throat. The first of many.

When they began screaming, Marion smiled. She would have known the sound anywhere.

A mother always knows.

THE MOM FROM UPSTAIRS
BY TEAGAN OLIVIA STURMER

Mom made puppets. My childhood memories are draped in pink neon fur, sequined fabric, dowel rods, and plastic eyes. Every holiday, every birthday celebration, *hell*, even most weekends were spent with my dad in the living room watching old reruns of *The Waltons*. At the same time, Mom's sewing machine whizzed away in the basement to the tune of her whistling the Beatles, "Run for Your Life."

I hated the puppets. Most, *thankfully*, didn't stay in the house. Mom got commission work from theaters in the city; her puppets were tucked gingerly into boxes and shipped. But the few that did stay—those of Mom's own imagination, so different from the ones people liked to see on stage—would watch us from the bookshelves in the living room, their hard eyes reflecting the mustard yellow shag carpet and my own face during the few times I had the guts to steal a glance at them.

Standing on the steps leading to the front door now, I freeze. God, I do not want to have to face a single damn puppet today. I shouldn't even be here. I should be at home, in Boston, with Mike and our stupid shih tzu, Reba. My hand tightens around the strap of my overnight bag. Mom sounded panicked on the phone. Like truly, *there-is-a-murderer-in-the-house*, kind of panic. She has always been level-headed; even after Dad died and she was left all alone to deal with the property, and the paperwork, and the funeral arrangements, she remained logical.

People die, Val, she told me. *Doesn't mean* we *stop living.*

I repeat those words as my hands reach for the doorknob.

But Mom's not even dead. She's just … God, do I even know what she is? She used the word *danger.*

Please come home, Valerie. I'm in danger.

I tried pressing her for more. What kind of danger was she in? And who exactly from? But she just kept repeating it over and over until I agreed to come home. Only for two nights, though. I was only going to stay for two nights. See what the deal was, what she was afraid of, maybe talk to a few of the neighbors I still knew. Maybe, I don't know, call a fucking psychologist.

But first, I need to actually walk *through* the door.

I wrap my fingers around the brass knob and stop. I should probably knock. In case Mom thinks I'm an intruder and comes screaming around the corner with a baseball bat or kitchen knife. I form a fist and rap lightly on the door three times. Silence. I wait. A minute goes by. Then two.

Okay, that *is* weird. *God, what if she is dead?*

I reach forward to knock again, and just as I am about to hit the wood, the door swings open. I teeter forward.

"Valerie, my darling!"

I regain my footing, gripping my overnight bag like there's no tomorrow, and look up. *What the hell?* Mom stands in the opening, the smell of stale smoke and lemon furniture polish wisping out around her. That's normal. Familiar scents from childhood, even though Dad has been dead for seven years, and I'm pretty sure no one's lit up a cigarette inside since.

No, what's wrong is ... well, *it's Mom*. Sure, it's been almost a year since I last saw her (she insisted Mike and I come for Thanksgiving, and *gosh*, how could I say no to overcooked turkey and the annual reminder of what a terrible, uncaring, distant daughter I am?) but I'm pretty sure I would've noticed if she'd been losing weight.

Mom opens the doorway for me to pass by and into the house. Her hair looks darker (could be dye), the wrinkles around her eyes and lips are smoother (could be Botox), and I'm pretty sure she's down at least three waist sizes (could be loads of things: healthier eating, a gym membership, a new doctor).

Her smile tightens. "Aren't you going to come in, sweetie?"

"I, uh, yeah." I stumble over my words stupidly and slip into the house.

Mom lets the screen slam and shuts the door. When she turns around, that smile is still plastered on her face. She reaches for my bag, and I let her take it, stunned by her appearance. I mean, she *looks* like Mom. But, like, maybe Mom when I was two? Not almost thirty-two.

"How was your trip?" she asks, dropping my bag on the autumnal-patterned velour sofa and waving me over to the kitchen table. "Coffee?"

I draw a blank, watch as she glides across the linoleum and fills the Mr. Coffee maker with tap water. I scan for signs of an intruder, of someone making Mom *act* this way. Like everything is fine.

"Uh, yeah, it was fine. The layover in Detroit took forever, but I brought a book." I step forward, *what am I even saying?* "Mom, are you okay? On the phone—"

The water gurgles in the glass pot as she spins around, eyes hard. There we go. There's that look. That *you abandoned me and look at what do you have to show for it?* look. Then it disappears, hidden beneath that shiny grin.

"Oh, that," she titters, filling up the coffee machine and dropping the pot down on the hot plate. "I'm so sorry about that. Woke up one night thinking I heard something in the house. Turns out it was just the cat!"

She scoops coffee grounds from a red metal canister and turns, a smile tugging on the corners of her lips like someone has attached thread and pulled. Hard.

My stomach fizzes. "Mom, we don't have a cat."

She laughs. It's a light and airy thing. Not the usual barking sound I'm used to. "Sure we do, honey. Remember, we got Mindy when you were ... seven? Eight?" She pulls two mugs down from the cupboard. "I'm sure it will come back to you once you see her."

I scan the living room, the same as it always has been. No cat in sight. Just the mustard shag carpet, a boxy TV tipping haphazardly on an old coffee table, the bookshelves stuffed with dusty tomes ... and puppets. I recognize most of them—the yellow and blue Bad Idea Bears from *Avenue Q*, a smaller version of Audrey 2 from *Little Shop of Horrors*, a few originals that dredge up nightmares of my dad scaring me to death by hiding them in my bedroom.

I look away. God, I can't stand them. They're so ... *wrong*. Like they are watching every move I make, waiting for me to mess up. Again.

The coffee pot starts spitting, and soon, Mom places a white Pyrex mug in my hand. *She still has these?* I take a sip; the syrupy liquid coats my tongue. Mom is at my elbow, eyes on me like she's waiting for some kind of approval. I lift the mug. Smile.

"Good," I say. "Real good."

We lag in awkward silence for a moment, and I wait for Mom to take a drink of her own coffee, but the mug just sits there in her hand. I blink. *Wait, her nails are painted?* I don't think I've ever seen my mom with painted nails a day in her life. They're a hideous shade of green. Like a cat threw up and—

A cat. I take another sip of coffee, look back toward the puppets. I think I would remember having a cat. Plus, if we got a cat when I was seven (or eight), wouldn't that make it ... twenty-five? That would be a scientific miracle.

"So, Mom." My words cut the tension in the air like a dull butter knife. "If you're fine, why am I here?"

One cat's puke-green nail clinks against the side of her mug. "Oh, just because I missed you. Can't a mother miss her child?"

So it begins. The guilt trip. I bite my cheek, take another sip of coffee. "Sure, Mom, of course. I just—"

"It's just that you never come home anymore, Val. And we miss you so much."

We? Something cold snakes up my back. I grind my teeth and try not to look at the damned puppets watching me from the bookshelf. She probably meant the cat.

There is no cat.

I drop my mug onto the table and sink back against the chair. "Look, Mom, I'm happy to see you and everything. And I'm glad you called me. I want to be here if something really is wrong, but you seem fine. I mean, hell, you seem more than fine."

Mom, who's still not drinking her coffee, sits down opposite me. "You want something *wrong*, Valerie? You left. You left, and you hardly ever come back, and you don't understand how hard it's been, how lonely—"

"God, Mom!" I drop my hand to the table and slosh the coffee in our mugs. "I went to college, I moved to Boston, I met Mike, I got a life. You know, most parents would be proud of their kids achieving what I have."

Everything goes quiet. Mom looks like she's trying to decide her next move.

Something rattles behind the basement door, and my eyes jerk to the dark paneling.

"I told you," Mom hums. "Just the cat."

My fingers tighten on the coffee cup. I want to tell her to shut up, to hell with this made-up cat, *why the hell am I here?* But I don't. I just turn back, take another breath. A big, deep one, just like my therapist taught me.

"Mom, look, if there's nothing wrong, I will have to go back home. I took off work to come out here and—"

"You push buttons on machines, Valerie. I think they can do without you for a few days while you visit your poor mother." She swirls her coffee around but doesn't take a sip.

I snap. "Are you kidding me? I'm a fucking *oncologist*, Mom. Do you know what that word means? It means I help people fight cancer. I give them hope when there is no one else to turn to." I push my chair away from the table and stand up. "This is ridiculous. I should have seen this coming." I march into the living room to retrieve my overnight bag. I only turn back to her when I reach for the door, and there she sits—perfectly calm, collected, one nail *tip-tapping* the side of her full mug. "Next time you get freaked out or decide there's some fake cat running feral around the house, call a neighbor. I'm out."

The kitchen floor creaks sharply. "Your birthday is tomorrow."

Mom's voice hits me like a ton of bricks. She remembers. *Of course, she remembers.* Except last year, she didn't call. Or the year before that. When I asked her about it, she said, "Why call your daughter when your daughter doesn't call you," even though I'd been on the phone ... because I'd called her.

"What does it matter to you?" I try to look anywhere besides at Mom, and my eyes land back on the puppets. The Bad Idea Bears wink ghoulishly at me. *Wouldn't you love to spend your birthday here with us? We could get up to all kinds of trouble.*

I don't think I need any more of that, thank you.

Mom steps toward me, and honestly, I'm surprised at how quickly she can walk. Wasn't it just last Thanksgiving she'd joked about needing to buy a cane? She closes the gap between us until I can see the bloodshot whites of her eyes. Those, at least, are familiar. Aged.

"I think you should stay," she says. "For your birthday. Let me do it all for you—presents, cake, decorations." She reaches a hand toward my cheek, and her skin is cold. Ice cold. My spine spasms. "Please, Valerie. Let me be your mother."

I should pull away. I should get back in my rental car, drive to the airport, book a flight, and go home to Mike and Reba and all my patients. But I don't. Because the way she says it, *be your mother*, it's like she wants a second chance. Maybe it's the fact that I want a second chance, too, or maybe it's because of watching too many people lose loved ones and carry regrets right out of the hospital with them, but I take my hand off the doorknob.

"Fine," I say. "Fine, but only until my birthday, and then I've got to go back home."

That funny smile tugs on Mom's lips again, pulling them so tight they turn pale. "Oh, Val. We're so glad."

She used that word again. *We. We're.* Who knows, maybe she's talking about the cat. Mindy. I flop down onto my childhood bed, the Rainbow Brite sheets still smelling of fresh detergent even though I haven't slept here since I was eighteen. I run one hand along their soft surface, and it takes me all of two seconds to bury my nose in them and start crying.

A second chance.

Part of me feels stupid for buying into it. Maybe my birthday will come, and Mom will forget. There will be no presents (who needs them, I'm going to be thirty-two), no cake (probably for the better, these jeans come with a high price), and no decorations (I haven't seen a crepe paper streamer since 1993).

But what if she does remember?

What if it's like I've always dreamed it would be? The birthday party I witnessed all my friends get but never got myself. I mean, *hell*, even the Bad Idea Bears got more love than I did.

I roll over and come face-to-face with my pink rotary phone. God, how long has it been since I last picked it up and dialed a number? I push myself into a sitting position and grab the receiver. I hold it up to my ear.

It's still connected.

A laugh cracks out between my lips. I should call Mike. Tell him I'm fine, Mom's ... fine, I'm just going to stay for a few days, and then I'll come home. My cell is probably buried beneath layers of clothes anyway. I dial the numbers I know by heart and wait as it rings.

And rings and rings and rings.

Hello, you've reached the cell phone of Michael Sorrento. Please leave a brief message, and I'll get back to you as soon as possible. Beep.

Of course.

I leave a quick scramble of thoughts. *Everything's good, sorry I won't be around for my birthday, we'll celebrate when I get home. Love you, bye. Don't forget to walk Reba.*

I drop the receiver back down and am about to stand up and unpack my things when I hear something scratching ... something *inside* the wall. My spine freezes, fingers go numb. What the hell? I wait until the silence has hollowed out my ears and stand up. It comes again. *Scratch-scratch-scratch.* My heart seizes, and I hold my breath. I drop to my hands and knees, scuttling across my pink carpet, and press the side of my face against the wall.

Scratch-scratch-scratch.

It's coming from the vent that leads down to the basement. I scurry away from the wall.

Just the cat, right? You know, the cat that doesn't exist. Sweat slips down my neck, and I reach to brush it away. And then the phone rings, jarring me. I have to bury my fist in my mouth just to keep from screaming. I strain my neck to look at the phone. *Why isn't Mom answering it?*

Thinking it could be Mike calling me back, I scramble up and pick up the receiver.

"Hello?"

A male voice crackles on the other end. "Hi, Mrs. Davis?"

"No, sorry, this is her daughter, Valerie."

The voice hesitates. "Right, well, this is Dr. Sievers. I've been seeing your mother for … quite a time now. Does she happen to be home?"

Something wet sloshes in my belly. "Yeah, she's home. Is there … is there something wrong?"

The line crackles, and I swear I hear someone draw in a long breath. "Well, unfortunately, I can't speak directly to your mother's condition, Ms. Davis. Patient confidentiality and all that. Could you tell her I called, though? She missed her appointment yesterday, and I'm—I'm just concerned, is all."

The wet feeling crawls up the back of my throat. I try to swallow. "I can go get her, Dr. Sievers."

"No, no. That's fine." His voice sounds timid now, almost scared. "Just, uhm, let her know I called. Maybe she can call Tracy, make another appointment."

Sure. Okay, make another appointment. Except, whatever has the doctor worried doesn't sound like the sort of thing to let wait until another appointment. It sounds like the sort of thing you'd pack someone into the car and drive them to the emergency room for.

"Uhm, sounds good. I can let her know," I say, the wet feeling now gobbing at the base of my tongue.

"Good, great. That's great. Thank you, Ms. Davis."

The line clicks.

Mom doesn't make dinner that night. Which is fine, she was never really a good cook anyway. I order in Chinese—crab wontons and sweet-and-sour chicken—and Mom and I plop in front of the TV for a *That '70s Show* marathon. I only realize Mom isn't eating anything when Eric, Donna, Fez, and Hyde slide into a table at the Hub.

"You're not hungry?" I ask, licking red sauce off my chin.

She turns to me, eyes bright. Smiles, the TV glare reflecting off her strangely white teeth. "Oh no, honey. I'm fine. You just eat as much as you like."

Weird, but okay. I take another bite as the canned laughter rings from the TV. "Your doctor called."

Mom tightens, her muscles going straight as wooden rods. "My what?"

I rip into a piece of dripping chicken. "Dr. Sievers? He said you missed an appointment—"

"I'm sure it's fine, Val. Just eat your food and enjoy the show." Her voice is brusque.

Part of me wants to argue, but now Eric and Donna are sitting on the hood of the Vista Cruiser, and so what if Mom has stopped eating? I'm only here for another day. Can't fix anything in one day. There is too much broken between us.

When we turn in for the night, Mom kisses me on the cheek and tells me she'll try and make pancakes in the morning.

"Oh, you don't have to do that, Mom. I'm sure I can scrounge up some eggs or cereal." This is me trying to be considerate—she doesn't have to get up early and make me breakfast—but it clearly rubs her the wrong way. Her eyes glass over, and her nostrils flare. Always a bad sign.

"I said I'll cook you pancakes, Valerie. Now go to bed, and I'll see you in the morning." She turns and disappears behind her bedroom door, leaving me in the hallway feeling like I'm twelve years old again.

Did she ... did she just send me to bed? God, she can be so controlling. I clench my fists and march into my bedroom, trying hard *not* to slam the door. I fish my pajamas from my bag and plug my phone into the wall. When it finally lights up, there are three missed calls from Mike. I should probably call him back, but I'm honestly so tired I could fall asleep on concrete right now, so I drop my phone to the floor and roll over in my Rainbow Brite sheets.

It's strange being back here with Mom. Maybe tomorrow will be better. My birthday. Cake, presents, decorations. *Pancakes.*

I'm imagining the taste of syrup just as I hear an echo from the vent near the floor.

Scratch-scratch-scratch.

Like the point of a needle.

My shoulders shoot up to my ears.

Just the cat, I tell myself. *Just the cat, just the cat, just the cat.*

I chant this until I drift off into some semblance of sleep, even though, for the life of me, I cannot remember owning a cat a day in my damn life.

The first thing I feel when I wake up is the pain. And then I see the blood. It stains my sheets in little red lines, and when I tear off my pajamas, I see why. Criss-cross scratches cover my body, neck to knee, like some grotesque game of Tic-Tac-Toe. I scramble back against the headboard, chest heaving, trying not to scream.

What the hell?

What the fucking *hell?*

I yank a shirt over my head and stumble into the bathroom, shutting and locking the door behind me. The water gurgles out hot, and I rub soap into my palms before scrubbing every bleeding inch of me. Honestly, I should jump in the shower, but I'm already here, and the water would sting more than it already does. Grimacing, I rinse the soap out of the cuts and dry off. I entertain the idea of Band-Aids for a moment, but there are so many little scratches I'd be covered neck to knee in bandages, and there's no way Mom has that many.

I go back into my room, the scent of flour, baking soda, and sugar intermingle with the stale cigarette smoke.

Mom's voice comes from the kitchen. "Val, that you?"

"One second!" I cry and hurry into a pair of sweats and an old band T-shirt.

Mom is standing in front of the stove when I come out, six perfectly golden pancakes on a Pyrex plate on the table.

"Happy birthday, honey." Mom practically sings as she brings over another cup of coffee and, to my surprise, a cake.

A real ass cake. Pink, covered in silver star sprinkles and thirty-two candles. What is happening?

She sings me the Happy Birthday song, makes me blow out the candles, then sits me down in front of the pancakes and watches me devour the entire plate.

"Aren't you hungry, Mom?" I ask, maple syrup coating my throat.

Her smile pulls back, all teeth. "Oh no, honey. This is all for you."

I eye the cake suspiciously. There's no way I can eat it all by myself. I get up to wash my plate, but Mom takes it from me.

"It's your birthday."

I plop back down. This is all so strange. This is like every dream and birthday fantasy I ever had wrapped into one, and yet something feels off. The noises from the basement, Dr. Sievers's call, Mom not eating, the fucking scratches on my body.

"Do you happen to know if the cat got upstairs last night?" I ask.

Mom doesn't look up from where she's scrubbing the plate. "What, honey?"

"You know, the cat. Mindy. Did she get upstairs last night? I, uhm." I take a swig of coffee. "I woke up covered in weird scratches, and I thought maybe she got out and into my room and, I don't know, attacked me?"

God, it sounds crazy when I say it out loud.

Mom stacks the plate on the drying rack beside a baking bowl and beaters. "I guess she must have."

Okay, well. That takes care of that, I suppose.

Mom's eyes dart to the basement door. "I stayed up all night last night working on your present, and it still isn't quite ready. Do you mind if I go down and work on it for a bit? I'll bring it up when it's finished."

I groan inwardly. The last thing I want for my birthday is some goddamn puppet. But I put on a brave face. "Sure, sounds great."

She grins, and I stand, walking toward my room.

"Valerie?"

118

When I turn back, I could swear tears are in her eyes.

"Yeah, Mom?"

"We're just so glad you're home."

There's a bad smell coming from the vent in my bedroom. It reminds me of meat and rotten fruit and dog shit, and instead of going down to the basement to tell Mom, I just shove my bean-bag chair in front of the vent and call it *good enough*. I leave tomorrow anyway. She can deal with whatever creature crawled in there and died.

Probably the fake cat.

I'm about to go to the bathroom to see if Mom has any Neosporin to put on my scratches when the phone rings.

"Hello."

"Elaine? This is Scott. I'm—"

"Hey, woah, sorry," I choke out. "This is Elaine's daughter, Valerie, who's this?"

The voice on the other end is silent for a moment, then clears its throat. "Oh, uh, this is Scott Trombley. I'm the director up at the Ordway Center. Elaine was supposed to get me my big Audrey 2 last week, but she never showed up. My actors have to use a tennis ball attached to a rod during rehearsals. We open next weekend, and I'm getting worried."

My stomach ties itself into knots. Mom has never once been late on a puppet order. I look back to the beanbag chair in front of the vent.

"She's down in her studio right now, actually. Let me go check on her and call you back, okay?"

Scott hesitates, and I'm pretty sure he's about to lay into me on the importance of deadlines in the theater, but all I hear is a "thanks, Valerie," and the line goes silent.

My palms go sweaty, thinking about trudging down into the basement. Mom never let me down there as a kid. I wipe my palms on my sweatpants and sneak out into the hall. There's a strange humming sound as I get closer to the door, and when I open it, I realize what it is.

Mom's whistling "Run for Your Life."

I stop short on the stairs, that raw beef smell hitting me in waves. What the hell is it? The sewing machine whirs, a scritch-scratchy sound, and Mom's whistling gets louder.

I go down another step, pulling my shirt collar up over my nose.

"Mom?"

The sewing machine stops. Something scuttles. A bulb flicks off.

"Mom?" I come down past the edge of the wall and blink. Rub my eyes. *What am I seeing?*

There's the usual: bolts of neon fur, plastic heads lined up on dowel rods, sequins and buttons, and elastic cord. Mom sits at her sewing machine, back to me.

"Just in time," she says, and her voice sounds wrong. Like it's coming out of her mouth but far away.

And then something slinks out from a shadow.

It's Mom. Another Mom. The Mom From Upstairs. Thin, young, bright. I look back at the mom at the sewing machine. The dusty gray-brown hair, wrinkled knuckles, the *ropes* tying her to the chair. *What the fuck?* And by the machine, a line of sewing pins, each point darkened with rust.

Blood.

My blood. The scratches.

"Mom?" The sound comes out cracked and broken, the concrete cold on my feet.

This is wrong. Something is wrong.

The Mom From Upstairs comes at me, a needle sharp and glinting in her hand. "Oh, Valerie, happy birthday. Your present is all done. Would you like to see it?"

I start backing up but trip on the stairs, going down hard. My wrist cracks, and I hold back a scream as Mom—not Mom—bends over, that wicked grin spread out like wet paint.

"We missed you. You moved away, and you left us all alone."

The puppets on the shelves—some done, some half done—turn their plastic eyes to me, and a scream gurgles in my throat.

"What—I don't understand."

The Mom From Upstairs is so close now, and I can see the eyes. So real. So familiar. But there's something else. Something in the skin that reminds me of thread. "She wouldn't do anything about it. *Elaine.* Said the past was in the past. But we missed you, Valerie. So, we built ourselves a body."

My wrist is throbbing. There are tears in my eyes. I look at the mom sitting by the sewing machine. Flesh and blood, Mom. She turns. Slowly, head cracking at wrong angles. And that's when I scream, when the noise rips from my throat. When I see that mom—the real mom—doesn't have eyes. Just bloody, raw sockets. Rotting flesh.

The Mom From Upstairs grins, the needle in her hand teasing my throat, my chin, the delicate jelly of my right eye.

"We want you here and for always with us, Valerie. We just want to play. Play, play, play. But you left. We were patient, but we couldn't miss another birthday. And now we'll have presents. Every day. All day. We won't be alone anymore. Elaine will be happy. Happy, happy, happy."

I try to scramble up the steps. A splinter of wood breaks off and embeds beneath a fingernail. I scream again, but it's no use. The Mom From Upstairs is kneeling on my chest, her wooden puppet leg a lance to my ribs. I can't breathe. God, I can't breathe.

The needle pierces my cornea, and I let out a scream. A bloody, wet cry. Something in the corner moves. Something made from wood and fabric and stained with what can only be blood. My blood.

It turns, and my jaw goes slack. Brown hair, tiny nose, an old band T-shirt strung on dowel ribs. Oh my god, it's me.

Its eyes are empty.

The Mom From Upstairs holds a plastic-smelling finger to my lips, sinks the needle in deeper, and all I can do is squirm and bite my tongue.

"Don't worry," she coos gently. "We've built you a body, too."

WITHIN THE PINK
PAISLEY WALLS
BY KELSEA YU

The magnolias were in full bloom the day Miralyn Liang found the envelope addressed to her, penned in her dead mother's hand. Tucking it in her dress pocket, she climbed back down the ladder, wincing as her bare feet hit the cold concrete of the garage floor. If Laura had been there, she'd have insisted that Miralyn wear socks or slippers. But Laura was upstairs resting again; she did that a lot now that the baby was almost here.

Though Miralyn had been looking for a book from her mother's boxed-up library, the envelope was a far better find. She tiptoed out of the open garage and padded across the front yard toward her favorite tree. Fuchsia petals fell as she climbed up to her usual spot and nestled in. It wasn't far off the ground, but she liked it here; the branch was curved like a chair, and she felt safe, surrounded by the blossoms her mother had loved.

Miralyn inhaled deeply, filling her nostrils with the scent of sweet, pleasant magnolia. Then she opened the eggshell envelope and slipped the contents out.

She had hoped for a heartfelt letter written the day she'd been born or, perhaps, a note of advice to guide her through the ages. Something to show that her mother was thoughtful and wise and possibly gifted with the foresight to prepare Miralyn for a motherless future.

What Miralyn held, instead, was a faded Polaroid.

She pored over the image, drinking in every detail. Her mother sat on a mint green tufted armchair, hands folded primly in her lap. Her head was tilted to one side, thin lips curved up in a closed-mouth smile, and she stared straight at the camera with eyes that shone bright. Behind her, the walls were covered in pink wallpaper, covered in a white paisley design.

Below the image, a handwritten address: 13 Cedar Boulevard.

Thirteen. Same as Miralyn's age. Laura said it was an unlucky number, though Miralyn's father didn't believe in such superstitions. Miralyn wondered what her mother would have thought.

The guilt arrived immediately, pitting in her stomach. It felt wrong to compare her mother with Laura, no matter how innocent the point of comparison. It felt too much like comparing old versus new, original versus replacement. Her mother was her mother, and Laura was Laura. There was no crossover.

Miralyn slipped the Polaroid into her pocket and went inside to look up the address on the family's shared computer.

The following day, Miralyn walked home from school, Laura's voice running through her mind. *Come straight home. Do not talk to anyone or stop for any reason. I'm serious, Miralyn. I want you to stay safe—both your dad and I do. We can't let you walk home alone unless you promise to follow these rules.*

Miralyn had promised. Those first few days, Laura waited on the porch each afternoon for her to arrive, face settling into relief when she caught sight of Miralyn.

But months had passed, and nowadays, Laura was usually dozing when Miralyn returned from school.

Miralyn stopped at an intersection. She knew she should keep walking, but her gaze slid right. *It* was only two blocks out of the way. Two blocks were barely anything. If she walked quickly, her detour wouldn't count. She would arrive home at roughly the usual time. And all she wanted was a look at the outside. What was the harm in that?

She turned right.

The house at 13 Cedar Boulevard might once have been deemed an adorable little starter home with its buttercup yellow exterior, white scalloped trim, and ivy running down the trellis. Now, it was a dilapidated thing, shrunken with age, windows and doors boarded up. The siding was pockmarked where the paint had peeled, the gutter sagged with rotting leaves, and overgrown ivy strangled everything.

Miralyn pulled the Polaroid from her pocket and held it up to the house in disbelief. She blinked and rubbed her eyes, willing the scene before her to change. The place her mother had led her to find could *not* look like this.

Miralyn was halfway to the front step when she started, staring at the words spray painted in poppy red on the boarded-up door. *NO TRESPASSING!*

When had she decided to walk toward the house?

Uneasy, Miralyn turned around. She tucked the photo into her skirt pocket and found her way back to her usual route.

She didn't know how long the stop had taken; all she knew was that she needed to return home before Laura woke up.

She picked up her pace.

Each night, Miralyn slept with the Polaroid under her pillow, and each morning, she carefully tucked it into the pocket of her outfit of the day. Her father had said her mother loved dresses and skirts with pockets, so that's what Miralyn insisted on wearing. Since Miralyn's mother had died when she was on the cusp of forming long-lasting memories, all she had were fuzzy bits here and there, which she filled in with her father's tales.

Before Laura, Miralyn's father had spoken of her mother often.

At school, Miralyn found herself doodling paisley patterns in her notes during lectures. In art class, she painted with rosy pinks and minty greens. On her walk home each day, she tried not to think about the house or the Polaroid. But it was like having someone place a slice of your favorite cake in front of you and tell you not to eat it.

Nearly two weeks passed before Miralyn gave in, making her way toward 13 Cedar Boulevard. As she approached, she was surprised to find the house looked both shabbier and less menacing than she'd remembered. In her imaginings, the vines had grown thorns, the curls of peeling paint resembled curved claws, and the spray paint on the door had turned dark as blood.

This time, Miralyn didn't stop to stare. She had already decided to break Laura's rule; might as well go all in. She stepped over a fallen section of fence on the side of the house and slipped into the backyard, hoping no one in the neighboring houses would notice.

Miralyn figured this would be a scouting trip. She'd get a closer look so she'd know what to bring next time to help her break in. But there was a loose board over the back door, and when Miralyn tested it out, it moved aside easily.

Miralyn stepped inside.

Other than the strip of light streaming in from her entry point, the house was dark. Something squeaked, then came the sound of something scurrying across the floor. She swallowed hard, recalling her history teacher's lesson on the Black Death, how rats bearing disease-ridden fleas had helped spread the plague. She shivered, nearly ready to turn back.

"Miralyn?" a soft voice called.

Miralyn jumped. Her elbow bumped the wall, hitting something sharp, and she gasped in pain.

"Miralyn?" The voice was laced with concern now. "Are you all right, dear?"

Gritting her teeth, Miralyn stepped backward, feeling for the loose board. She wanted to turn and run, but her skin crawled at the thought of turning her back on whoever—or whatever—was in the dark house.

"Miralyn, you're bleeding. Let me take care of you."

As if her thrice-repeated name was an incantation, Miralyn stopped in her tracks. Her eyes must have adjusted because now she could see the barest outline of a small kitchen table and three matching chairs. Up ahead, a sink and stove cut into the speckled countertop. And beyond that, a glow in the distance.

Miralyn couldn't remember why she'd been afraid. This was why she had come, to explore the little house. She stepped toward the soft light into a hallway.

Framed photographs hung on the walls. It was still too dark to make out most of the details, but Miralyn thought she could see a pair of gleaming eyes in one of them, the silhouette of three figures in another. Ahead, light spilled out from beneath a closed door. Miralyn made her way down the hall. She turned the handle, and the door creaked open.

The room inside was small and achingly cozy. In person, the pink paisley wallpaper was softer, less disorienting, and the velvety armchair looked like something you could sink into for a long, leisurely nap. A hand-carved mango wood table sat beside it, and the wall boasted a fireplace.

"Sit, my dear, and let me tend to your wound." The voice seemed to emanate from all around her. Miralyn liked the way it spoke. The words felt antiquated, reminding her of the historical fiction she'd found in her mother's collection.

"Who are you?" Miralyn sat. The armchair was even comfier than it appeared.

"Why, don't you know, Miralyn?"

Miralyn. It pronounced her name just right. She hadn't had to correct it. She couldn't remember the last time someone had said it correctly the first time. She was seven months into the school year, and one of her teachers *still* called her Marilyn. "How do you know my name?"

The voice laughed, a melodic sound like the ringing of Christmas bells. "Well, I was the one who named you, of course."

Miralyn sat up. "That's impossible."

The voice tutted. "Impossible is such a limiting word, isn't it? Now, hold your arm out and close your eyes, dear."

It occurred to Miralyn that there was one way to find out who the voice really belonged to. Playing obedient, she held out her arm and closed her eyes. She felt something brush her arm, the slight pressure as her shirtsleeve was rolled up to expose her elbow. Curiosity bubbled up within her, but she forced herself to wait another moment to ensure they were distracted.

"Relax, my dear. This will only sting for a moment." Something wet and squishy pressed into Miralyn's elbow, and she drew back.

"What is *that*?"

"Only a sponge, dearest."

It felt too squirmy and ticklish to be a sponge, but she didn't argue. Silently, she counted to thirteen. Then she opened one eye a fraction to peek.

There was no one there.

Maybe they were hiding just outside her peripheral vision. She tried to turn her head ever-so-slightly to get a better look, but her lashes kept blurring everything.

"All cleaned up, dear."

Miralyn opened her eyes all the way. She was alone in the room. "But … where did you go?"

"Here, of course. I'm always here. Now run along, darling, or you'll be missed. But come again soon, won't you? It's lonely here, and you've been such good company."

"I …" Miralyn wanted to ask more questions, but then she thought of what would happen if she came home late. Laura would be frantic, calling everyone in the school directory. Thanks to an incompetent cervix, she'd been ordered on bed rest, which meant Miralyn's father would have to start leaving work early to pick Miralyn up from school. That meant reducing his hours, which they couldn't afford with the baby coming.

If she came home late, everything would fall apart, which would be Miralyn's fault. She would lose her freedom of movement. She might not be able to return here easily.

And she found that she did want to come back.

"I'll visit soon," she promised.

Miralyn thought she caught a glimpse of a smile in one of the patterns on the wallpaper before she left, closing the door behind her.

Outside, she inspected her elbow, pressing on the spot she'd torn open. It was still tender, but the gash was sealed up, the blood gone.

The morning after Miralyn's visit to the house, Laura went into labor, and Laura's mother came to stay with them to help with the squalling thing.

Miralyn knew she should be helping out more. She wanted to be helpful. Her father was busier than ever at work—his boss had laughed when he'd inquired about paternity leave—and baby Riley seemed to need something every other minute.

It was just that Riley was so *annoying* and *gross*. He woke Miralyn with his screaming in the middle of the night, and he was always covered in some distasteful substance of his own making—drool, vomit, urine, excrement, flaking skin—that inevitably ended up absorbed by the clothing of whoever was nearest. Plus, whenever Miralyn tried to hold him, making sure to support his little neck with her forearm, she could feel

Laura hovering, ready to snatch him back at the first sign of an imperfect cradling position.

Miralyn had thought Riley would be a good distraction, making it easy for her to slip away. But Laura's mother kept a vigilant eye, busy as she was. Miralyn dared not do anything but walk straight home from school each day.

It wasn't until Laura's mother flew back to her home across the country that Miralyn finally had the chance to visit the little house again. By then, a month had passed.

"Miralyn, dear, where have you been?"

"My baby brother was born. I had to help out." Miralyn felt bad lying, but did it really count if the person you were lying to was, themselves, a liar? They *had* to be.

"Your ... baby brother?" Something sharp lay beneath the soft edges of their words.

Miralyn colored, remembering who the voice had claimed to be. "My baby *half*-brother. Dad, um ... wants me to call Riley my brother, but I know he's not really, y'know, my full brother. That would be impossible."

"That word again. Well, darling, I missed you." The voice lingered on *missed you*, all the sharpness gone. Miralyn let the words wrap around her like a warm hug. She smiled, setting down her backpack.

"I brought some things for the room." She pulled out the goodies she'd gathered. First, she strung up the fairy lights, taping them to the pink wallpaper and then flipping on the battery pack. Second, she took out a thin travel blanket and set it on the armchair. Last, she took the extra peanut butter and jelly sandwich she'd snuck into her lunch bag the night before and set it on the side table.

Miralyn sat on the chair, laid the blanket on her lap, and picked up one half of the PB&J. "The other half is for you."

"How considerate you are, my Miralyn!" The voice sounded delighted.

Miralyn waited, feeling mighty clever. If the voice belonged to someone, they would have to show themselves in order to eat.

No one showed up.

"I brought the sandwich for us to share. Can we eat together?"

"Of course, dear! Close your eyes and take a bite, Miralyn, and I'll do the same."

Miralyn frowned. "I don't usually eat with my eyes closed."

The voice sighed. "Me neither. But it's only temporary. Soon, we'll be together for real, mother and daughter. The way things should've been."

Miralyn's intake of breath was audible. "But …"

"In the summer, we'll sit and read together under the shade of the magnolia—the big one in front of our house. It was my favorite tree when I was … more corporeal."

"We'll … read together?"

"Surely, you didn't think your love of reading came from your dad. That's all my side of the family. When you were a toddler, your favorite time of day was bedtime because that's when I'd read you a story."

In an album Miralyn had pored over countless times, there was a photo of baby Miralyn snuggled up against her mother, who read from a board book.

"And we'll bake together! I'll teach you the recipe for matcha thumbprints, my favorite cookie."

Miralyn tried to imagine this. Her mother moving back in with her and her father.

And Laura and baby Riley.

"Okay." She closed her eyes and took a bite of her sandwich. From the side table, she heard the sound of munching.

Miralyn began visiting the house on Monday and Thursday afternoons. She'd told her father and Laura that she had joined a biweekly study session with friends from school.

Each time, she brought more treasures and snacks to share. And when Miralyn wasn't there, the voice did its part, dragging in furniture from other parts of the house and cleaning them up for use. Soon, the pink paisley room had a little library, a second armchair beside the fireplace, an assortment of cozy blankets and floor pillows, and a coat rack. Below the fairy lights, Miralyn had hung up her paintings from art class and photos taken from an album she'd found in her mother's boxes.

Miralyn had begun to believe the voice might really belong to her mother. She knew too many things about Miralyn's life and childhood that she couldn't have known otherwise, like Miralyn's first word (*more* as in *more food, Mama*) and the way the third step from the top on the main staircase in Miralyn's house always squeaked.

Gone were the days when Miralyn had to slip through the gap in the fence, exposing herself to curious neighbors' scrutiny. Nowadays, she took a more discreet route that led directly to the backyard of 13 Cedar Boulevard.

Miralyn pushed aside the boards and walked through the dark, dusty house the way she always did, headed for the pink room. She opened the door, a wave of happiness settling over her. It was peaceful here. No squalling baby.

"Hello, dear." Miralyn's mother always sounded so happy to see her. It was a nice change from her father's tired nod after a day at the office or Laura putting a finger to her lips and mouthing *Riley is asleep*.

"Hi, Mom! I brought some of your old clothes, like you asked." She opened her backpack and took out a floral dress, brown sandals, and a wide-brimmed sun hat. She laid the sandals on the floor, then hung the hat and dress up on wall hooks. Her fingers accidentally brushed the wallpaper, which felt slightly squishy and oddly warm.

Miralyn drew her finger back, inspecting the spot. For a moment, the paisley teardrop resembled an eye. She blinked, and it was just a random shape again.

She had caught glimpses of this from time to time—a slight shift in the wallpaper pattern, the barest hint of an ear, or a curved upper lip. She didn't pay it much mind; it was far from the strangest thing about this place.

"Shall we continue reading your book together?" Miralyn's mother asked.

"Yeah!" Miralyn opened *Horrid* to the bookmarked page and set it on one of the armchairs. Then she curled up in the other chair, opened a pack of Bin Bin Rice Crackers, and covered her eyes with a sleep mask. She snacked as she listened, careful not to crunch too loudly lest she miss something.

Miralyn's mother had a beautiful, sonorous storytelling voice. When she read aloud the conversations between Jane and her mother, Miralyn could almost imagine both characters were there in the room with them. Miralyn let the story envelop her, picturing the details captured so vividly on the page.

When the chapter was finished, Miralyn pulled the sleep mask off, walked over to her mother's armchair, and picked up *Horrid*. The seat was still warm. She placed the bookmark in the new spot and closed the book.

"Time for you to run along, dear."

Miralyn sighed. "I wish I didn't have to leave."

Though the fireplace remained unlit, warmth tickled Miralyn's cheeks, and she heard the crackle of logs burning with a phantom flame. She imagined her mother smiling.

"You have no idea how much I wish you could stay longer, Miralyn. I love you, darling."

"Love you, too, Mom."

It was a sunny Thursday, and school was almost out for the summer. Miralyn took her usual shortcut down a side street and through the neighborhood park to the house on Cedar Boulevard. As she approached, she heard voices. It was probably a neighbor, but it didn't hurt to exercise caution. Nervous, she crept up to the backyard and peered through a hole in the fence.

Two strangers in hard hats, goggles, and reflective orange vests inspected the board she usually pushed aside to enter. One said something to the other, who jotted it down on a clipboard.

Miralyn couldn't make out their words over the roaring in her ears.

The thought of them going inside—*had they gone inside?*—and finding the pink room sent a wave of panic through her. She fought the urge to run up to them and shout at them to leave the place alone. It was *hers*. Hers and her mother's. They were trespassing.

But what would she say? She didn't own the place, nor did she know who did. She forced herself to take three deep breaths and listen.

"God, what a shithole."

"Yeah, the ones that've been empty awhile always are."

"What's the story here anyway?"

"Owner died, kids couldn't decide what to do with it, blah blah. One of them tried fixing it up, but y'know how these old houses are."

"Money pit."

"Yep. They finally decided to sell it, but squatters had moved in by then, and it was a whole mess. Took almost a year for them to sort it out and find a buyer."

"Well, they're doing the right thing, knocking this place down. Some places aren't worth salvaging."

The roaring in Miralyn's ears was back. She pictured a wrecking ball tearing through the pink room. Ripping the fairy lights off the wall and smashing the little corner library she'd worked so hard to curate. She imagined herself walking through the wreckage, calling out. Listening for a voice that never came.

She had just found her mother; she could not lose her again.

Miralyn watched and waited, but the workers kept walking in and out of the house, assessing various things.

At last, Miralyn tore herself away. She had to get home before her father or Laura suspected. She had to figure out what to do.

Miralyn had never snuck out before. Her nerves rattled as she tiptoed through the silent house, taking care to skip the creaky step on her way downstairs. The room shared by her father and Laura—and Riley, now in his little bassinet—had a window facing the front, so Miralyn figured going out the back was less risky. Sneakers in hand, she unlocked the sliding glass door, wincing as it made a little *pop* sound, and squeezed through the opening. Carefully, she slid it shut, put on her shoes, and headed for the yellow house.

Between the moon's glow, the occasional streetlamp, and light spilling out from windows, Miralyn was able to find her way. This time, there was no board to push aside to slip inside; the workers must have taken it down.

Moonlight seeped in through the hole in the boards, casting strange shadows on the living room. Miralyn shivered. She had grown accustomed to how the house felt on warm afternoons, but being here in the dead of night was different. The cool air shimmered with possibilities, and she half expected a clawed creature to leap at her from the shadows. She walked briskly down the hallway, opening the door to the pink room.

Inside, it was dark.

Worry caught in Miralyn's throat. Though she hadn't known why or how, the pink room had always had its own illumination.

"Hello?" Miralyn wished she'd brought a flashlight.

For a moment, the room flickered with a faint pulse of light, and she glimpsed a shadowed figure standing slouched by the fireplace. She jumped.

"Miralyn?" The voice was faded, weak.

"Mom?"

"I had to keep … this room … safe. Hidden from those … men."

"What?"

"It's hard … to maintain … this shape." The light pulsed brighter this time, revealing a woman in the outfit Miralyn had brought over. Her black hair was cut in a bob, just the way it looked in photos Miralyn had seen of her mother. The woman's eyes glistened. She wobbled, then slid down the wall, hitting the ground with a thud.

Miralyn rushed forward. "Mom!" The room grew dark again just as she reached out to grasp her mother's arm. Her fingers sank into her mother's skin, and she screamed.

"Sorry … dear. Trying to stay … corporeal."

"What do I do?" Miralyn could hear the panic in her own voice.

"Help me … move my … nest."

"What?"

The light pulsed again, and this time, her mother's face was only inches away. Miralyn could see something wriggling in her mother's pupils, and the skin of her face was all wrong. It was lumpy and shifted oddly, as if things were squirming beneath the surface, trying to escape.

Miralyn took a step backward, fear clogging her throat.

Her mother reached out a hand. "Miralyn … help me."

"What are you?" Miralyn whispered.

"I'm … your mother." Hurt laced the woman's voice.

The light went out, and Miralyn sucked in a sharp breath. It was pitch dark, and her eyes hadn't adjusted. She tried to turn toward the door but wasn't sure where it was.

"Help me." The words tickled Miralyn's ear, and she screamed, shoving wildly. She heard a crunch as whatever the creature was hit the ground. Then, the horrible sound of something tearing open, like fabric being ripped apart, followed by a gurgling noise and the skittering of a million tiny feet.

Something crawled up Miralyn's leg. She screamed, batting it away, but more took its place.

Another pulse of light illuminated the room.

Inches from her foot, there was a pile of a rough, unevenly textured beige fabric. It was bursting with little white centipedes, wriggling their way toward her. They were between her and the door.

"Miralyn," her mother's voice wailed.

Miralyn looked down. There was a bump in the fabric, shaped almost like a nose, and hair attached to it; black and short, like the bob her mother had worn ...

Bile rose in Miralyn's throat. She wanted to close her eyes and scream until someone came to rescue her. She missed her father, Laura, and even baby Riley with a fierceness she'd never felt before. She wanted to be curled up in her own bed at home, wrapped in her favorite blanket.

But no one else was here. No one was going to save her. If she wanted out, Miralyn would have to save herself.

"Be brave," Miralyn whispered. She swallowed hard. And then she screamed, leaping over the mass of wriggling things and the fabric-that-was-not-fabric. She grabbed the door handle, using all her willpower to ignore the little things she could feel crawling up her legs, their twitchy little feelers probing into her socks. She pulled the door open.

"Miralyn, help me," her mother said again.

At the sound of the voice, Miralyn turned back reflexively. The room was still glowing, but the light wavered unevenly, frantically. Before Miralyn shut the door, she noticed one last thing about the pink room—the white paisley pattern was gone.

Back at home, in her room, Miralyn combed every inch of her clothing and shoes. She did her best to think of anything but the pink room as she wiped centipede guts from her hair and wrapped half-smashed insect bodies in tissues to throw out. She didn't understand what had happened at the house and wasn't sure she wanted to know.

Miralyn was exhausted. But every time she closed her eyes, she saw her mother's face, little insects wriggling beneath her skin. Heard her mother's voice, pleading and desperate.

"You survived," Miralyn told herself. "Everything turned out okay."

When she fell asleep at last, her fists were clenched, her pillow wet with tears for the mother she would never have again.

"Miralyn!" Laura wrapped Miralyn in a huge hug. "How was school?"

Miralyn hugged her back. Several weeks had passed since the night she'd snuck out, and she'd been slowly warming to Laura. She wasn't sure why she hadn't been able to fully embrace her stepmother before. She now realized how kind, patient, and caring Laura had been. Laura worried more about Miralyn's safety than her own father did. Laura was exactly the mother she needed. "It was good."

"I'm glad." Laura smiled, but it looked strained. She cleared her throat. "So, I don't want to discourage you from being artistic or anything. You know I fully support your hobbies. But, uh … I was in your room this morning to grab laundry, and I noticed your design. It's pretty, but, um, do you mind just … not painting on the wall? I can get you some canvases if you'd like."

Miralyn blinked. "I didn't paint on the wall. Why would I do that?"

Laura frowned. "I don't think it could've been anyone else."

"Where was it?"

Heart pounding, Miralyn followed Laura up the stairs. When Laura moved Miralyn's hamper to reveal the patch of wall behind it, Miralyn already knew what she'd see. Still, she stared and stared.

There, on her turquoise wall, was a perfectly painted, beautiful white paisley swirl.

LITTLE MOTHER

BY LEE MURRAY

my first baby was Patricia
blonde hair styled after the queen
and her arms and legs crabbed inward
I scribbled on her face with a ballpoint
it blurred like an old tattoo
I didn't play with her after that

then came Lee, named after me
long black hair and blinky eyes
it was around the time I discovered scissors
I cut her hair to bristly tufts
and the winky eyelids, too
she didn't look so good after that

then there was a doll from China
dressed in slinky silk brocade
pink cheeks and a tiny rosebud mouth
painted and perfect on porcelain
her fabric limbs were limp and lifeless
even before I cracked her face open

Buffy was my next charge
red plastic curls and permanently naked
when her arms and legs detached
I pumped her torso full of tap water
Dad glued the limbs back on, and the bitten-off foot
but she was always stiff after that

Still later, I remember a Barbie
(I bent her legs backward)
and a cabbage patch dolly
(I pummeled its stomach)
and Marcie, a soccer mascot
(but by then I'd given up kicking around with dolls)

All that was years ago
I'm expecting a real baby now
I don't see why any of this is important?

[*Attachment Doll Play Assessment (ADPA) provides a helpful
framework for the study of developmental competencies,
including future emotional and behavioral well-being.]

BUTTONS
BY EMILY HOLI

I do not know where I live. I do not know what the trees on my street look like if there are trees at all. I do not know what color my house is painted on the outside. I do not know my neighbors' names, voices, or faces. *Je suppose* I do not know much.

But I do know a few things.

I do know that the sunlight spreads across the living room floor in the morning and creeps down the living room wall *la nuit*.

I do know that lentils taste better with salt than without. I ate salted lentils once. I remember those salted lentils *très bien*.

I do know that wishing for things is a silly thing to do.

I do know that *Maman* loves buttons.

I do know that, on Tuesdays, *Maman* goes to *le marché* for *pain et fromage*. I do know this because, on Tuesdays, *Maman* says, "*Je vais au marché acheter du pain et du fromage.*" Sometimes, *Maman* also buys *fleurs*. She keeps them in a vase on her nightstand. I love when *Maman* comes home with *quelques fleurs de toutes sortes*. She does not like it when I touch them.

I am a very good girl.

When *Maman* goes to *le marché*, I am alone for most of the afternoon. If I had a doll to play with—*peu importe*. I read books instead and talk to my tiny potted tree, *Annette*. She is tall

147

and skinny, like me. She does not answer, but I know she hears me. *Annette* is a very good listener.

Réellement, I like to be alone. When I am alone, I can do as I please—a little. I can jump up and down. I can stretch my arms and legs and move from side to side. It feels good to jump up and down, stretch my arms and legs, and move from side to side. I like the way it feels. No one has to know.

It is Tuesday afternoon, and I am telling *Annette* about the dream I had last night. A dream about a big, dark *trou*. In my dream, *le trou* was wide and deep, craggy, and steep, and someone inside of it was calling my name.

> *Charlotte*
>
> *Charlotte*
>
> *C h a r l o t t e*

And in my dream, I walked closer and closer to *le trou*, even though I was scared. Closer, and closer, and closer, until I was balancing on the edge of *l'obscurité*. I inched and leaned, and the rim began to crumble, and I started to fall—

> *f*
>
> *a*
>
> *l*
>
> *l*
>
> *l*
>
> *l*
>
> *l*

And then I woke up.

I am showing *Annette* how I fell, but I lose my balance and fall to the living room floor instead. My fall makes a very loud sound. Shuffling to my feet, I shiver, sure that *Maman* is coming to scold me. But then I remember that *Maman* is at *le marché*, and I am alone.

I dust myself off. *Annette* is frowning at me, as usual. *Annette* worries too much.

I am fine.

I brush the front of my jumper, but as my fingers flit across the shoulders, I shiver once more. *Non.*

My jumper is missing a button. It must have fallen off when I was telling *Annette* about *le trou.* "Nothing good happens *se tortiller*," *Maman* always tells me. She does not like it when I wiggle about. *Maman* is right about most things.

I must find that button.

I search under *la chaise*, but I do not find my button. I search behind *Annette*, but I do not find my button. I search under *le tapis*, but—I do not find my button anywhere.

Maman gets very angry when I lose things. I do not like it when *Maman* gets angry.

But then, *j'ai une idée.* As I did say, *Maman* loves buttons. In fact, she collects them. Hundreds of buttons of all shapes and sizes. Pearly white. Greasy bronze. Smooth wood. *Clair comme de l'eau de roche.* She keeps them in her special button box.

"*Boutons, mon chere*," *Maman* tells me whenever she finds a new button. Then she reaches under her bed, pulls out her special button box, and places the button inside of it. "But, *nous n'y touchons pas.*" And I do not.

C'est vrai. I do not usually touch *Maman's* things, but I do need a new button for my jumper. I can sew it on myself. I can help. I am a very good girl. No one has to know.

I reach underneath *Maman's* bed and find the special button box. It is dusty on top, with deep grooves carved into the sides. I have never held the special button box in my hands before. *Prés*, it does not look like a box a person would keep buttons in, but I open it anyway. From the corner of my eye, I see *Annette* frowning at me, drooping her branches to tell me she is nervous. But I ignore her.

I am fine.

I am a very good girl.

I search through the box, careful not to make a mess. The box is *remplie* with lots and lots of things. I find lots and lots of buttons. I find other things, too.

I forget that I am looking for buttons.

I find letters. Some are from a person called *Suzanne*. Others are from a person called *Louis*. Both people call me *sœur*. Both people call me *manquante*. One letter talks about *Colmar*, about *les coquelicots* in the springtime, bright and silky and pink, the smell of the *Rivière Lauch*, and the sounds of the *ville animée*, and I wonder, and I smile. I cannot remember the last time I smiled. This makes me shiver, too. I shake my head from side to side, and my smile falls to the floor like my lost button.

I find pictures. Pictures of people laughing, jumping, *en train de jouer*. None of the people have shaved-bald heads. None of the people have short-cut fingernails with bright red tips. None of the people wear gray jumpers with two gold buttons. None of the people look like me. None of the people look like *Maman*.

I find two dolls—one pink, one *blue*. I have never had one doll before, let alone two. I pick them up and hold them in my hands, but then I see—the dolls have *étrange* buttons for eyes. *Noire profond*. The buttons are sewn with thick red thread. They do not look like dolls *jouer avec*. I wonder more.

Mystere.

I hear footsteps behind me, slow and heavy. Shivering again, I close the special button box and slide it back under *Maman's* bed, but I know. The front door clicks. A heavy *manteau de laine* shuffles, and the metal coat stand clangs in the hallway. There is no time to leave. There is no place to hide. The thick, heavy smell of *pain et du fromage* fills the air.

I know it is too late.

I turn and find *Maman. Il n'y a pas de fleurs.* She walks past me, slow and heavy, *silencieuse.* She reaches under her bed and gathers her special button box because she knows, too. Somehow, *Maman* already knows.

"*Boutons, mon chere,*" she whispers. "*Mais tu l'a touché.*"

Maman is right. I was not supposed to touch.

"*Ferme tes yeux.*"

Maman opens her nightstand. She grabs her pointy sewing needle and a spool of thick red thread. I wonder about *les coquelicots* in the springtime, the smell of the *Rivière Lauch,* and the sounds of the *ville animée.*

I glance at *Annette.* She is frowning, as usual.

Then I close my eyes and wait.

I am a very good girl.

I do not know where I live. I do not know what the trees on my street look like if there are trees at all. I do not know what color my house is painted on the outside. I do not know my neighbors' names, voices, or faces. *Je suppose* I do not know much.

I do not open my eyes again.

I do not find my missing button.

But I do find *le trou.*

SPECIAL MEDICINE
BY MEG HAFDAHL

Memory squeezed at my guts. It was the smell, some floral-scented spray mixed with shit. I didn't want to remember. Every part of me thrummed with the effort of forgetting. I grabbed a mint ChapStick from my crossover bag and dotted its waxy head beneath my nostrils.

"Smell getting t'ya?" Angel, the night nurse, watched from the bedroom doorway. Squat and confident, she filled the entire frame. "I don't smell much of anything anymore. Thank the lord."

I gave my best fake smile, all teeth. "It's not so bad."

"Uh, huh." Angel squinted at a morning sunbeam that had cut across the front bay window, refracting down the corridor to land on her wide face. "It's past my bedtime."

"Yeah, sorry." The venti Starbucks mocha in my hand felt suddenly conspicuous.

Angel sighed. "A pretty typical night. Restless. Going on about her noises."

"Okay."

She moved away from the door, shuffling past me to get to the front, where her argyle-patterned raincoat waited on a hook. "When's the last time you were in?"

I wanted to take a sip of the mocha that made me late. But I resisted. "Oh, um …"

"That long?"

Shame heated my cheeks. "Work." I squeaked.

The wrinkles of Angel's forehead worked into a knot. "You don't have to wait to visit for times like this when the day nurse calls in sick." She folded her coat over her arm. "Your mom doesn't have many days left."

I swallowed the bitter mucus pooling at the back of my throat. "Sure, yeah. I know." My fake smile returned, bigger than ever. "Thank you, Angel."

"Hmm, just saying." She picked up her tote bag beside the door, Tupperware banging inside.

I turned into my mom's room, closing my eyes until I heard the screech and crash of the screen door. That, too, brought unwanted memories like ugly little gifts at the base of my brain.

"Emmie?" It was a wet and foreign sound.

"Mom." My eyelids pushed open, forcing me to see her. Mom was in the hospital-grade bed with side rails, her stringy hair stuck to the pillow with sweat. She was skinnier than before and curved in like a brittle comma. Her skin was the color of bile.

"Where's Angel? Or … or Linda?" Mom clutched at the frayed edges of her quilt.

"Angel needs sleep, and Linda has the flu." Finally, I took a long, luxuriant sip of my mocha.

She coughed, wiping the spittle on her chin with a feeble, claw-like hand. "Oh."

We lingered in the silence. In the sick-person stink.

"Could I have more water?" Mom gestured to a plastic cup on her side table.

I nodded, setting down my Starbucks as far from her as possible. "That cup, it's got to be twenty years old." It was a faded neon green with FERRIS HOSPITAL printed on both sides.

Mom watched as I picked it up. She gave what I guess was a smile. "Oh yes … probably got it when you were … what seven? Eight? Remember Ferris? Awful hospital, really. Gave us the runaround."

"Nope." Childhood chew marks decorated the cup's rim. "Don't remember."

The bathroom, the very same one Mom and I shared for eighteen years, emanated a hellish new scent that threatened to co-mingle with the bedroom. My throat slick with mocha-flavored mucus, I decided to ditch the Starbucks once I returned to Mom. Next time: black coffee. Or something like mint tea to soothe the nausea.

The clamshell sink long ago faded to a sickly salmon, was cluttered with medications and a drying enema bulb. I twisted the oxidized knob, filling the cup with cool water. Daring a glimpse into the mirror, I was pleasantly surprised to see I was indeed a grown-up and hadn't tripped back into the past. I wasn't in my Barbie nightgown, thin hair in tufts, pale and miserable.

I had color in my cheeks. Mascara.

The scar from my childhood port poked out of the top of my blouse. I set the plastic cup down and buttoned my collar. In a sort of ritual, I felt compelled to check my other scars. I rubbed a thumb down my side, where my feeding tube had once protruded. Fingered the thick tissue at the base of my neck where there had been a hole in my trachea. Aside from dressing like the urban legend of the girl with the green ribbon tied around her neck, there was no hiding that one.

As I reached to grab Mom's water, a loud *crash* sounded from the kitchen. I turned, holding my breath so I could hear more.

"Emmie!" Mom screeched from her bed.

I held still.

"Emmie! It's them!"

Them?

"Linda? That you?" I walked out of the bathroom's open door and down the short hall. "Feeling better?" *Please, God. Then I can fake a work emergency and get out of here.*

That sense came, you know when it feels as if someone's sharing your air. The space around me got heavier. But when I stepped into the kitchen, there was no one.

A stack of paper plates and plastic spoons had fallen from the counter onto the linoleum. A light load for such a heavy crash.

I kneeled and scooped up the mess, reminding myself that Libby, our one-eared cat, had died eight years ago. And she hadn't been one for kitchen counter shenanigans anyway, as Mom would spray her with a bleach bottle if she dared.

"Is it them? Oh!" Mom started coughing.

Them.

Mom had talked about *them* before. Interlopers in the house. Both Linda and Angel had assured me this was normal dementia fare. The sort of vague, paranoid hallucinations that come with your brain turning to Swiss cheese.

How quickly she could twist from lucid to confused.

Just as I turned from the counter to head back to get Mom's cup, I spotted another fallen item. I'd missed the piece of paper, which had curled beneath a lower cabinet. I knelt again, somehow still sensing as if someone, maybe even Libby, the dead cat, was in the kitchen with me.

A drawing. Basic crayon. Only a few different colors and probably done with nubs rather than good, sharp ones.

ME + MOMMY

Mom had a huge head, stick arms, only three fingers, and bangs. That's right. She'd had bangs then. Curled and sprayed to hell.

And I was just like Mom in the drawing but a bit smaller. I'd even drawn a crude rendering of an IV trolley lingering behind me like a ghost.

Unlike Ferris Hospital, which I'd lied about not remembering to Mom, I really couldn't remember this drawing. Doing it. Or even seeing it around the house before. After I stood and set it back up on the counter, I felt wax on my fingers.

Fresh crayon, the color of blood.

A long day of caretaking slowly bled into night. We ate black bean burgers together for an early dinner. Mom complained about the patty being too squishy, though she ate every bite. We watched reruns of *Family Feud* on the iPad set up on her dresser. Mom giggled at pretty much everything Steve Harvey did.

The sound of her laugh made me think she could get better. That maybe she would get out of bed and throw a load of towels into the washing machine. Dust off her long-forgotten cross-stitch projects. And then I'd look away from Steve Harvey to study her gaunt profile. Her lips sank back into her mouth. Her smile was haunting, alien. The thrust of her top teeth when she laughed, insincere. She laughed because that's what the TV audience was doing. Her eyes were gone. Covered in a snotty film. She was not here in her stinking bedroom with *Family Feud*. She was in the stark confines of her mind.

I glanced out the window, surprised to see the streetlights flash on.

"Mom?"

"Hmm?"

"What time does Angel usually show up?"

"Angel?" Mom stuck her ring finger in her mouth and sucked.

"Don't." I handed her a thin napkin from Chip's Takeout.

She ignored the napkin, sucking louder. Her tongue swished around her knuckle, searching for salt.

"Jesus, Mom. Angel? Does she come at eight? It's eight o'clock now."

Her eyes, searching balls of slime, stared into mine. She let go of her finger with a wet *pop*.

"Your first dose is at six. Remember?" she asked.

I shook my head. "No ..."

"And then feeding tube at eight. Bath at nine. Dose again at ten for good measure. Before the doctor comes."

"I'm not sick anymore." That churning nest of memories spoiled in the bottom of my belly. "You are."

I stood up from the dining chair I'd dragged in beside her bed.

"I am? I'm the sick one?" It was the cloying voice of a corny little girl, like a bad Shirley Temple impression.

She even fluttered her eyelids as if she had long, impressive lashes.

"I'm gonna call Angel. See when she's getting in." *And then I can leave and drive across town, drink a bottle of red, go to bed, and forget all of this.* Tears actually welled at the thought.

"Oh!" Mom tilted her head, scraggly hair tickling at the sweaty bend in her neck. "You hear that?"

I strained my ears. Finally, I heard the *whoosh* of the refrigerator opening and then the *rattle* of jars in the door as it closed.

"She's here." Mom slid down into the cocoon of her sheets. "Make her leave."

"Angel helps you—"

"Not Angel." Heavy tears rolled into a puddle in her ear. "Please, Emmie. Please. She scares me." The sheen had dissipated from her eyeballs, making them appear veiny and frantic. She wagged them back and forth, from me to the door, to the window.

"Okay." I reached out to pat her bony hand, but she flinched. "There's nothing to be scared of, Mom. I'll go see."

"No … no … no …" Her frightened gaze cut right through the flashing commercials playing on the iPad. "She's scary."

Thankful to leave her, I gulped fresh air in the hallway. A shadow cut across the kitchen light into the hall, and I was sure I was going to hug Angel for relieving me.

"Hey—" The rest fizzled on my tongue like a bitter Pop Rock. Instinct made me wrap my arms around my struggling stomach. I wanted to ask who she was, this woman at the counter. She wasn't Angel or any nurse.

My nausea turned into a swampy fear. It mired my feet into invisible sludge. Held my hands firm.

The woman, dressed in acid-wash jeans and a faded pink T-shirt, turned from her task at the counter. I knew Garfield would be on the front of her shirt, smiling with his white, blocky teeth. And I knew the woman's bangs were curled and sprayed to hell.

When she regarded me, this woman who existed thirty years ago, she grinned. An authentic smile, the kind she always gave me right before she injected a dose of my "special medicine."

"Mom?" I croaked. She was young. Frighteningly vibrant. It wasn't possible, and yet it was her.

The fear tightened like hardening clay around me, gripping my muscles, filling my veins with lead.

I wanted to ask how. How had I walked into the past? Or had she walked into the future? How was she dying in the bedroom while her younger self was in the kitchen?

What came out of my trembling mouth was, "What?"

Perhaps in answer, she picked up what she'd been stirring at the counter. A small, clear Tupperware container.

There was another tumultuous flip in my belly at the mixture inside. Brown and slopped up on the sides, the smell was unmistakable.

The ghost of my mother, as human as me, walked toward me with her plastic bowl of shit.

Please! Please! Stop!

The cries resounded in my head, but I couldn't make them come out of my feeble mouth.

Just like then. Just like I was five years old and sick and unable to speak.

She breezed by me, solid as any person. The smell wafted, and an unwelcome burst of pain thumped between my eyes.

I had to stop her. This was my chance.

The place where my port had been, my feeding tube, and the breathing apparatus in my neck, they all thrummed like fresh wounds.

Fear trickled into a distinct panic, and I swiveled back toward the hall. My young mother lingered outside my childhood bedroom, then moved on toward the master. I ran, catching up to her as she passed the threshold into her own room.

My mom of now, vulnerable and dying in her bed, began to scream. It was an unnerving caterwauling that intensified my headache.

"EMMIE! Stop her! Please!" She thrashed weakly beneath the white sheets. Her quilt a ball on the floor.

Her younger self stopped at my mom's bedside. She set the bowl of shit down on the side table where I had recently finished my black bean burger. This detail wanted to ruin my sanity.

I bit at the flesh of my lips, watching my two mothers goggle at each other.

"Please, Emmie, she's making me sick," Old Mom wailed.

"Hush now, this is your special medicine, dear. It makes you better!" Young Mom slipped an unwrinkled hand into the waistband of her jeans and pulled out a syringe.

The sight of it made vomit tickle the back of my throat. I pressed my eyelids together, listening as she dipped it into the poop and drew up the watery sludge into the needle.

She became more discreet about it later when I was ten or eleven and started to ask more questions.

When I was five, she would do it right in front of me. And I would accept it. I would let her inject literal shit into my IV tube because she was my mother.

Because I trusted her.

Finally, the puke came. I hunched over and let it out all over my socks.

Old Mom's cries brought me back to the room. "No! Emmie! Help! I don't like it."

I righted myself, working to stay up in the mess at my feet. "Neither did I." I wiped my lips with the back of my hand. "I didn't like it either."

"Don't be ridiculous." Young Mom pulled the IV tubing toward her with the precision of a doctor. "You liked being sick and staying home with Mommy." She glanced at me over her shoulder. "We got so much attention. So much special care from the doctors."

Old Mom nodded. As scared as she was, she had to agree.

"No." I flexed my fists, unable to stop the anger threading through me like a patchwork of fire. "NO." My scars itched.

"Emmie!" Old Mom was back to simpering. Her bottom lip jutted out, an ugly, flaccid thing. "This time, she's going to kill me. I know it, I know it, I know it."

I took a step toward them. Vomit seeped into the fabric of my socks. I realized as I looked down at the chunks of my dinner, that I felt better. That my stomach felt quieter than it ever had.

I wasn't sick anymore.

"Mom." I looked past Young Mom into the eyes of the other. I wanted to recognize the darkness, the pain, the betrayal that I had known for so very long. "It's time for your special medicine."

Young Mom injected the foul contents into the IV line. Old Mom howled and then settled down into her death bed, oddly content. Still alive for a while.

Shaking, I stepped backward into the hall. Young Mom was becoming blurry. More like a proper ghost with fuzzy edges.

The door of my childhood bedroom squeaked open. A vivid, happy little girl stuck her head out.

Me.

Yet, she was unmarked with scars, her skin a pristine alabaster. Her eyes fresh. There was no squeal of the IV trolley behind her.

We smiled at each other, matching grins.

A BROKEN INHERITANCE
BY RENEE CRONLEY

Her maternal image distorts
as I grow into her features
and take my first steps into myself.
Her mouth becomes a tool
as she artfully drills a space
in my developing young mind
to fill it with a version of herself
that she could never attain.
I can't push her expectations out,
they weigh more than she says I do,
and my flaws are slights against her.
She throws her words out like stones,
pelting me with my failures,
tiny bleeding wounds in my self-esteem
that never have time to heal.
I can see them in the mirror,
staining my reflection repulsive;
I cry to wash them away,
but the damage is written on my face.

I see people read them like ink blots
trying to analyze what's wrong with me.
I can see them on other girls' too.
The ones who take the worst turns,
end up in the papers—
the public giving them a voice
after it's too late to use it.
Most of us live in the lead-up,
a suffering that doesn't make headlines—
just cycles.

DOG MOM
BY RACHEL HARRISON

The sun hovers over the playground like a great, watchful eye. I remembered a hat for Charlie but forgot one for myself. I take a small sip from her juice box. It's organic, but it tastes like sugar water to me. Organic sugar water.

I set the juice box down and pick up a packet of Goldfish. Whenever I get asked, I always say the best part about being a nanny is the snacks, an excuse to eat like a four-year-old. Most of the time, I'll get a laugh, but once someone—some woman— said, "Shouldn't the best part be the children?"

This happened at an ex-boyfriend's work holiday party, hosted at some dull, stuffy restaurant downtown where men took their wives, not their mistresses. Under other circumstances, I might have responded with a grin and a simple, "No." But I wasn't sure who the woman was, what she did at the company, or if she was this ex's boss, so I said, "Of course! I was only joking."

The truth is, both are lies. It's not the kids or the snacks. It's the money. That's the best part.

"Hi, Nicki!" It's Holly Keller-Clarens. These Westchester wives all have hyphenated last names. Holly is dressed in head-to-toe athleisure that I'm certain is from a luxury brand I've never heard of. She sets her Birkin down on the bench next to me.

"Mommy, can I go?" Her daughter, Kennedy, is maybe the most beautiful child to ever walk this earth. Kenny is well-mannered and well-dressed, always clean. She's adopted, and she was adopted because Holly has two college-aged sons and was bored; Holly likes to act like she's saved Kenny from some horrible fate.

Maybe, but I doubt it.

"Sure, baby. Go find Charlie."

"Thank you, Mommy!" Kenny says, skipping off toward the slide. Charlie sits at the base, playing with mulch. She likes to make hearts out of mulch. She likes to show me her hearts made out of mulch.

"Look, Miss Nicki, look! Look!" she'll say.

And I'll say, "Wow, so pretty! Very good!"

And I'll think maybe she'll be a sculptor someday, an artist. Maybe she'll defy her white-collar criminal defense attorney parents and go to a liberal arts school and learn about, like, Marina Abramović and move to New York City with her trust fund money and create something beautiful or subversive or both.

Or maybe she's just a stupid kid playing in dirt.

I have no skin in the game.

"Nicki!" Charlie shouts.

"Yeah?"

"Kenny is here!" The two hold hands and giggle.

"I see!" I say, giving her a thumbs up.

"We're going on the slide!"

"Great," I say. "Go for it."

My no-nonsense approach was one of the reasons Charlie's parents hired me.

"We want someone compassionate and gentle but who speaks to Charlie like a person, not a pet," her mother, Jamie, said to me.

"I think it stunts their growth," I'd said, because I believe it, but mostly because I knew it was what she wanted to hear.

"Well, you don't have the formal education," she said, pausing long enough to make me sweat, "but your references all spoke very highly of you."

"There's only so much someone can tell you about caregiving," I'd said. "Experience is everything."

I barely graduated high school, started babysitting for my cousin, and now I live in a mansion in a gated community and get paid a hundred thousand dollars a year to hang out with a preschooler.

All the playground moms are obsessed with me. They think I'm fascinating because I care about none of the things they care about, that they agonize over.

"I'm absolutely exhausted," Holly says, wiping the bench before she sits down. "We're heading to New Haven for Carson's game this weekend, and I haven't even packed."

"Still haven't found a replacement for Maggie?" Maggie was her live-in maid, who became her live-in nanny and maid, who got fired for smoking weed in her room. Rookie mistake.

"It's impossible to find good help," she says. "The good ones are all taken."

"Nicki! Nicki, look!" Charlie shouts from the top of the slide. "Watch me!"

"I'm not watching," I say, turning my cheek. "You shouldn't care if I'm watching."

She huffs but then goes down. I watch her out of the corner of my eye. I do watch. Of course, I watch. It's my job.

"You have such a unique approach," Holly says. "You're a perfect fit. For Charlie. With Kenny, she needs extra attention. We have to ensure she knows she's part of our family as much as RJ and Carson."

"Do you worry about overcompensating?" I ask. Another reason the playground moms love me is because I'm honest. Not as honest as I could be or want to be, but honest enough. They think I'm edgy and fun, and if I ever say anything they don't like, they get to leave the conversation still feeling better than me because they have *money*, money, and I don't. They're my livelihood. I need them. They have all the power.

"How do you mean?"

"Do you think if you're too precious with her, she'll feel alienated? That she'll eventually realize she's receiving special treatment because she's adopted," I say, stealing another sip from Charlie's juice box. "Even if she's being treated well. Is she being treated fairly?"

Holly narrows her eyes, pinches her lips, and plays with her Tiffany locket. Something I've said doesn't sit right with her. She'll get over it. There's no one else on the playground on Thursday mornings, so she has no one else to talk to, and she loves to talk.

Besides, out of all the mothers, she's the one who savors this power dynamic the most. She doesn't need me as much as I need her, but she does need me.

"Oh, look," she says, scoffing. She lifts her chin and gestures lazily to the paved path on the opposite side of the playground. "Dog Mom."

Dog Mom is a woman in her sixties, maybe, whose thin, frizzy hair is dyed orange, who wears neon leggings and fuzzy coats year-round, who wears hot pink blush and purple lipstick that's always smeared. Her spindly lashes are coated in too much mascara. She wears big, geeky sneakers and pushes a dog stroller carrying a yappy Pomeranian.

She's perfectly pleasant, always smiling and waving, but she scares the shit out of the kids. The playground moms all make fun of her. Treat her like a spectacle. Gossip. Sharon Hartford-Landy claims she heard a rumor Dog Mom encouraged her dog to bite a little boy. Bianca Phillips-Wood swears an unnamed source told her Dog Mom only ever buys dog food at the grocery store, that she eats the same food as her dog, sharing dishes of Cesar's beef in gravy.

I don't approve, but I also can't defend Dog Mom.

She shuffles down the path. Her mobility isn't great. It'll take her a while to get by. She's gotten the attention of Charlie and Kenny, who stand at the top of the slide with their fingers in their mouths, ogling.

Then Charlie drops her hands and squeezes her little fists together like she does when she's determined, when she's decided to be brave, and she goes down the slide. Kennedy follows her, and they march hand-in-hand over to Dog Mom.

"Kenny, honey!" Holly calls.

"Let them say hi," I say. "Conquer the fear."

"That dog could be rabid, for all we know," she says. "That woman is clearly not all together."

"I'm sure the dog isn't rabid. And she's just eccentric."

The girls wave to Dog Mom and point to the stroller. It's blue and has mesh over the carriage. I can't hear the conversation;

we're too far away, but the girls are smiling, and Dog Mom is smiling. She reaches over and pulls back the mesh.

Then the screaming starts.

Charlie and Kenny start wailing. Kenny runs away, toward us, toward the bench, but Charlie has gone rigid, frozen in place.

I'm up, sprinting across the playground to her, to my Charlie, so fast I could be flying.

"What is it?" I ask.

Charlie points to the stroller, unable to speak through sobs.

I look down and see that lying still inside the carriage is a dead-ass dog.

A small Pomeranian corpse swarming with flies and gnats. Its fur is matted, its eyes are rotted out, and it reeks.

I realize I can't remember the last time I heard this thing bark. It was always barking; how did I not register when it wasn't? Did my brain just fill in the blanks?

I pull Charlie to me, turn her head away. I notice her hat is off, gone missing, lost on the playground somewhere.

"What is it?" Dog Mom asks me, eyes wide and full of blissful ignorance. "Did Tootie growl? She's a sweetheart, I promise. Just a little nervous around new people."

She doesn't know. How does she not know?

"Charlie, why don't you go to Miss Holly?"

Charlie shakes her head. She won't leave me.

I sigh. "Miss, I'm afraid your dog is dead."

"What?" she asks, and there's something in how she asks. Her tone, her body language. I understand that she already knows and is in some deep state of denial. Or grief.

"It's okay, miss. It's going to be okay. All right? It … this happens. I'm sure your dog is … in a better place." I'm talking down to her, and I hate it. I'm trying to be gentle, but I sound condescending.

Dog Mom shakes her head. "You're mistaken. Tootie is just fine."

I put my hand on her shoulder and look her right in the eye. "Tootie is dead. Gone. I'm sorry."

I watch it happen. I watch her denial crumble. I watch her delusion fail.

Now, she's the one wailing. She goes around to the front of the stroller, falls to her knees as she sees what's inside. Really sees it. She reaches out and starts to pet it. What was once Tootie.

"I'm sorry," I say again, picking up Charlie and carrying her back to the bench where Holly is just getting off the phone.

"I called the police," she says.

"Why?"

"Someone has to deal with that. We can't have psychopaths on the playground traumatizing our children. I *told* you."

I look back over my shoulder, over to the path.

"My baby!" Dog Mom screams, cradling the dead animal in her arms, rocking it back and forth, back and forth. "My baby."

"Her baby," Holly says, clicking her tongue. She's given Kennedy a KIND bar and her iPad, and she seems fine. "It was a dog. Not even. A golden retriever is a dog. A German shepherd is a dog. That was a fuzzy rat."

Her lack of empathy is so staggering that I'm ashamed to know her, to be sitting next to her. To have ever spoken to her, associated with her. I've never been more disgusted by anything in my entire life.

"That *is* her baby," I say, setting Charlie down on the bench next to Kenny. "To her. That's her baby."

"Maybe. Only because she doesn't understand what it is to be a real mom."

"What does it mean to be a real mom?" I ask.

"It means you're the caregiver of a *child*," she says, sensing my indignation and becoming defensive. She has to be right; it's part of being better.

"I'm the caregiver of a child. Am I a real mom?"

"To be a real mom means you're with your child day in and day out."

"I am with Charlie day in and day out. I got her up this morning. I'll put her to bed tonight."

"It's not the same. Charlie has a mother."

"Dog Mom was with her dog baby day in and day out," I say, so angry I don't care that this isn't a fight worth having. Especially not in front of the kids. "How is that not a real mother?"

"She didn't give birth to her dog!" she says. "Being a real mother means you've given birth."

My jaw unhinges, falls to my feet. I scoff. "Okay, then."

Holly realizes her mistake, and her expression becomes mean. "You're a little ... a little ... you're a smug little bitch!"

I'm surprised, and frankly impressed, that she'd call me that.

"I'm sorry you feel that way," I say.

Holly grabs Kenny. "We're leaving."

They stomp off, leaving Charlie alone on the bench, sniffling.

"I'm so sad," she says.

"I know," I say, sitting on the ground in front of her, leaning an elbow on the bench. If I adopt a casual posture, she'll calm down. Kids pick up on these things. "Can you tell me why? Why are you sad?"

"That dog is dead. And that lady is sad. And Miss Holly and you were yelling."

I lift my hand to her forehead, shielding her eyes from the blazing, relentless sun.

"It is sad that her dog died. She's very sad about that. So sad, she wishes it never happened. She's having a hard time accepting that it did. Do you understand that?"

"I think so," she says, picking up my half-eaten packet of Goldfish. "She loved her dog, and she's sad."

"That's right. She loved her dog. She wasn't ready to lose it. And Miss Holly said she shouldn't be so sad because it's just a dog. That made me angry because I think we love what we love how we love it, and other people don't get to tell us that our love isn't valid. Does that make sense?"

Charlie shrugs.

Within the next hour, I know Holly will make a call to Jamie and put in a complaint that may or may not get me fired. I have no power over that.

A cop car pulls into the parking lot. Dog Mom is on the ground, clutching Tootie to her chest. The sound of her grief louder than any siren.

Charlie climbs down off the bench and into my lap, and I hold her, petting her soft, soft hair. Maybe I don't know what it means to be a real mom, but maybe I don't give a flying fuck.

I know what it is to love. There can't be more to it than that.

SOMETIMES, IT'S HARD TO LET GO
BY CAITLIN MARCEAU

Cerulean blue parts waves of black,
the water warm like childhood,
as Anna rinses away the shampoo
—sweet like spun sugar—
from her daughter's hair.

Her daughter watches her with wide eyes
—eyes passed down to her—
that used to smile and light up
whenever she'd see Anna,
back when she was innocent and small.

They were the same eyes Anna had,
ones that had looked for monsters under beds;
that had bored holes through school-yard bullies;
that had always let her daughter know she was loved.

The same eyes that had watched her grow
from an obedient girl on her first day of school,
to a stubborn young woman going off to college;
a hatchling that wanted to abandon the nest.

The same eyes that had watched her daughter
—her *beloved* daughter—
from behind closet doors
as she settled into her new home;
that watched from the back seat of a hot car
as her little girl went on dates;
that watched her child from beneath the bed
when she was intimate with boys.

Anna dries her daughter's hair
and braids it down her back,
the same way Anna's mother did for her
when she was just a child.

She runs the towel over damp skin,
careful not to upset the stitches
that keep her mouth shut,
and her daughter's wounds closed,
that mark where her limbs once were.

Her daughter watches with wide eyes,
a hostage in her mother's life because
—as Anna told her all those months before—
"Sometimes, it's hard to let go."

NEVER LOVE, NO ROOM
FOR MONSTERS
BY JILL BAGUCHINSKY

"Slow down!" My mother leans forward in the passenger seat and paws through the designer bag tucked next to her sensible heels. Blood trickles from the gash near her hairline, dribbling down toward the floor mat. "You always drive too damned fast. How many times do I have to tell you?"

"Ma, I'm at like fifty-eight. Speed limit here is fifty-five."

"Speeding is speeding. I would think you'd want to be extra careful these days." She cuts her remaining eye in my direction. "Considering."

I spread the fingers of one hand over my swollen belly like a shield and lighten the press of my foot on the gas pedal, letting the car slow to fifty-five. I hate to admit it, but she's not wrong. Not about this.

"Keep your hands on the wheel, Alice. Ten and two." When she sits back, the flap of loose, ruined skin on the side of her face flops down like a limp slice of lunchmeat, revealing hints of cheekbone and molar. She lights a cigarette.

"Ma, I've asked you not to do that in my car."

She takes a drag, and a whisper of smoke escapes from the hole in her cheek. "It's your own fault. You and your driving. I need to calm my nerves." She flicks ash out of the open window.

"Jesus, Ma, it's wildfire season. It's dry as hell out there."

"You know damned well that doesn't matter." She glances at me from the corner of that one remaining eye while what's left of her mouth pulls into a broken smirk. "These days, I can do whatever I want."

"Yeah, yeah." I sigh. *Like you haven't* always *done what you want.* Still, it's not like her glowing ash could actually ignite the dry grass. A cinder has to exist to start a fire, just as her cigarette would have to exist to stink up my car. I almost think I can smell it, but no. My last car, the Toyota I totaled on the interstate, carried the ghost of her smoke in its upholstery, even though I only drove her around in it for a few weeks before the crash. The odor had settled in quickly. My new Hyundai, on the other hand, is smoke-free. Blood-free, too, despite that dripping gash on her forehead and the matter congealing in her empty eye socket. "I know, I know. But still. Could you not?"

"Mind your business."

I keep my gaze focused on the road ahead and resist the urge to throw her a sharp glare. She's not serious, right? She can't be serious. The idea of my mother—my nosey, nagging, won't-leave-me-in-peace-even-when-she's-dead-and-rotting mother—telling anyone to mind their own business is …

Well, I don't know if it's ironic—Alanis Morissette confused me for life on that one—but it's definitely *something*.

She takes another puff. "Anyway, like I said, it's your own damned fault."

"Is there anything that *isn't* my fault?"

"What's that supposed to mean?"

My fingers tighten around the steering wheel. "You're not exactly obligated to ride around with me, you know. If my driving is so terrible—"

"And just what else am I supposed to do? You know I don't drive."

You could go into the light. Or straight to hell, I don't care.

"You know who was a good driver?" she asks, and my shoulders knot as I prepare myself for what's coming. "Charlie. Charlie was a fantastic driver."

Eyes burning, I swallow against the sudden obstruction in my throat. The sound of his name always hurts, but it hurts most when it comes from her. "Charlie was fantastic at a lot of things."

"I still don't know what you did to drive him away."

The air leaves my lungs like I've been kicked in the chest. "Nothing, Ma," I say softly, even though I know it won't do any good. "I didn't drive him away. He—"

"I know, I know. He *disappeared*," she says derisively, raising her hands to make air quotes. The move causes her cigarette to drop a clump of nonexistent ash near the gearshift.

"It's true."

"Honestly, Alice. You and your monster stories. Will you *ever* get tired of being so ridiculous?"

"You never believed me." My voice wobbles. "Not even when I was a kid."

"Can you blame me? The way you went on about monsters under your bed—it was so childish."

"I *was* a child!" I yelp.

"You can drop that tone right now." Ma's voice thins.

I bite back the shrillness, but I don't stop talking. I can't, not once I'm on this brittle, wounded track. "I was five, Ma. *Five.* Mr. Fluff disappeared when I was *five.*"

"That damned teddy bear," Ma mutters. "You never let anything go, do you? You left him somewhere. Dropped him in the supermarket or something. You always insisted on dragging him wherever we went; it was a matter of time."

"I was *five,*" I say again, fighting the catch in my voice.

"Children are careless." She pauses to cough. It's a sound I know well: phlegmy and thick, almost gooey.

I choke back a gag. "You'd think that would go away now that you're, you know …"

Ma clears her throat. "Some things are stronger than death." She sounds almost proud.

I sigh. "I know you don't believe me. You didn't then, and you never will. But I heard them, Ma. I heard those things under my bed. And when Mr. Fluff fell that day, I saw him get yanked under the dust ruffle."

"Nonsense."

"And when I was eight, and I found that kitten—"

"You left the window open. It got out. That's what cats do."

"She didn't go out the window. She went under the bed." I remember the absence of sound. Princess was mewing; then she stopped, all at once, leaving a silence sharp and keen enough to open a vein. "She went under the bed, and then she was gone."

"I think you've actually convinced yourself that's how it happened."

"I was heartbroken over that cat, and all you did was tell me it was my own fault that I lost her."

"What else was I supposed to do?"

"Believe me," I said quietly. "I needed you to believe me."

Ma huffs out a harsh breath. "What you needed was to get yourself under control and take responsibility for your own mistakes."

My own mistakes. For as long as I could remember, the sounds I'd heard coming from under the bed in my childhood room—the starving grunts, the gnashing teeth, the clicking and ticking of talons against the wooden floor—had somehow been my own fault, at least according to my mother. I was imagining them, and if I really didn't want to be scared, all I had to do was *stop.* The simplicity of her solution was cruel, especially late at night, when I'd lie awake, terrified and frozen as the things that lurked just below me began to stir.

I couldn't escape them until I moved out and rented my first apartment. Ma said it was gross sleeping on a mattress on the floor. She said no self-respecting adult should want to live that way.

I loved it. There was no room underneath for monsters. They could stay in my childhood bedroom. They could stay with Ma.

For the first time in my life, I knew truly deep sleep. I knew a different sort of silence—not the grim kind that followed the disappearance of a kitten, but a tranquil quietness that I hadn't realized was possible. That silence lulled me, and oh, did I sleep. I slept, and I breathed with lungs that no longer knotted and ached, and I made myself two promises: I would always keep my mattress on the floor, and I would never love anything or anyone ever again.

The teddy bear, the kitten—the monsters took everything I dared to love.

They never bothered taking Ma.

"Come home, Alice," she said over the phone now and then. "I'm lonely. I miss you."

I made excuses. I stayed away. As much as I could, I avoided her, and when I couldn't, I made myself numb and gray in her presence. I lived for myself, and I kept my promises. For years, I observed them like religious doctrine. Never love, no room for monsters.

Then I met Charlie. Charlie, with his bashful smile, and his soft voice, and that one lock of brown hair that tumbled over his forehead no matter how hard he tried to tame it.

I held out for as long as I could. I hardened my heart and refused to acknowledge its flutter. But my heart was patient, and so was Charlie, and finally, I broke my promise and loved him. He indulged my mattress on the floor habit so kindly and openly that when he finally nudged—gently, gently—I gave in and let him buy us a bed. I insisted on a platform bed, something heavy and sturdy with no space underneath, and he indulged me once more and found one that was perfect. He pulled me from the floor, from the spot to which I'd resigned myself, and I began to trust that my love for him was enough to keep us both safe.

Every night, for the better part of a year, we shared that bed. Every night until the one during which I woke to those old sounds—the grunts and snarls and clicking, ticking talons, coming from an impossible space beneath the solid platform. I reached for Charlie and found his side of the bed empty.

I never saw him again.

"Come home, Alice," Ma said over the phone when I broke—snapped in half—and made the mistake of calling her. "You need your mother, now more than ever." I let her gather me up and reabsorb me. What did it matter? The monsters were everywhere.

After a few weeks, during which she wouldn't stop suggesting that I had driven Charlie away, I aimed my old Toyota at the wall of an interstate underpass and floored the gas with her in the passenger seat.

I spent a few weeks in the hospital, and I have some scars now, but I lived, and I never let on that I'd crashed on purpose. There was a dog in the road, I said, and I swerved to avoid it.

In the hospital, I found out about the pregnancy. One last whisper of Charlie that the monsters couldn't steal, and I'd nearly snuffed it out myself. Somehow, somehow, our tiny wisp of a someday-baby survived the crash, too.

Ma didn't, but she stuck around regardless. I couldn't escape her. I never will. She stays with me everywhere, broken and ghoulish and complaining about the food I choose to eat, the clothing I wear, my driving. She bleeds and drips and smokes and criticizes.

"Have you given any more thought to that weight loss program we saw on TV the other day?" she asks, flicking the butt of her cigarette out the window again.

"Ma, I'm *pregnant*."

"I know that, Alice. I'm not an idiot. I meant for once you give birth. Pregnancy absolutely wrecks your figure. I was a perfect hourglass before you ruined me."

I grit my teeth and exhale. "My figure is the last thing on my mind."

"Fine, let yourself go. See if you ever find another man."

"Jesus, Ma! Just—" My words dissolve as my midsection squeezes and cramps like someone's wringing me out from the inside. "God. *Ouch!*"

"What? What is it?"

"I don't know. I think …"

"The baby?" she snaps. "It's too early for that."

The vise inside me won't let go. "We're not far from the hospital." I puff out a breath. "I think I should get checked out."

"Honestly, Alice. You're so dramatic. It's probably just gas."

I ignore her and make the turn.

The baby is early but perfect, and I give her the name I chose as soon as I knew she was coming: Charlotte. I see so much of Charlie in her eyes. She tore herself from me, fierce and tiny and flawless and screaming, and I've never loved anyone more.

That's what scares me.

I knew it wouldn't take long for the monsters to come, and I was right. I hear them now, the grunts and snarls and clicking, ticking talons under my hospital bed.

They sound so very, very hungry.

Ma dozes in a chair nearby, snoring softly, now and then phlegm-coughing in her sleep. Even the dead need their rest, it seems. Her head tips sideways, and the lunchmeat flap on her cheek falls open again, letting that leering side smile peek through. If it weren't for that, the oozing forehead gash and the rest of her ruined face, she would look almost peaceful.

She doesn't deserve peace.

"Ma! Wake up." I keep my voice low; I have a plan to carry out, and the last thing I need is a nurse overhearing and finding me snarling at an empty chair.

Ma groans in annoyance and opens her remaining eye. "This had better be important."

"Listen." I prop myself on one elbow and point under the bed. "Don't tell me you can't hear them."

Ma frowns. Her forehead—what there is of it—creases, and that trickle of blood finds the crease and navigates it, oozing sideways. "All I hear is more of your nonsense," she says, but I catch a hidden crack in her voice, and that's when I know.

"You *do* hear them," I say.

"I don't know what you're talking about."

"You always have, haven't you?"

Ma tosses her hands up in exasperation. "All right! Fine! Yes, I hear ... something. Are you happy?"

"You always knew I wasn't lying."

"I wanted you to be strong," Ma says, pulling out a cigarette. "Like me."

"Strong?"

"I heard them when I was young, same as you. I heard them, and I learned to ignore them. I wanted you to do the same."

"So you left me to them."

"So you could learn!"

Shaking, I swing my legs over the side of the bed and wonder if something will reach out and grab my ankle. "Goddammit, Ma. I was so afraid."

"Everyone feels afraid now and then, Alice! The point is to get over it. To be stronger than the fear."

"What you showed me wasn't strength," I say, standing, ignoring the soreness perching low in my newly hollow belly. "It was neglect."

"You'll see. Once that baby's old enough to come to you crying over every little thing, you'll understand why I—"

"That won't be happening." It's time. I've been planning this since I found out about Charlotte. I knew the monsters would come for her because I knew how much I would love her, and I wasn't about to leave her as vulnerable as I had always been. Getting the legalities in place without Ma catching on was tricky, but I let her think the paperwork was about Charlie's disappearance and the uncertainties he left behind. I never let on that it was actually for Charlotte—ensuring that she'll be safe and sound and cared for if I don't come back.

I don't expect to come back.

The monsters won't have Charlotte. I won't let them. They won't hunt her. They won't haunt her, and neither will my mother.

I'm going to war for my daughter and I'm taking Ma with me. She needs to face what she spent so long denying.

I reach for Ma. We haven't touched since long before her death, so I'm unsure whether what I have in mind is possible. She looks solid enough, sloughing old blood and flakes of decay onto the hospital floor, but can I actually grab her? Relief blooms in my chest when my fingers wrap easily around the clammy, graying skin of her wrist. The cigarette falls from her hand as I yank her to her feet.

"What do you think you're doing?" she demands as I pull her toward the hospital bed.

I drop to my knees and force her to do the same. "I'm breaking the cycle."

She recoils. "Let me go."

"No."

"This is insane." She paws at my fingers with her free hand, but my grip holds firm. "Think about your baby," she says, her tone thinning with panic. "Think of what you're leaving behind."

Like I can think of anyone or anything else. I wish I could say goodbye. I wish I could see Charlotte's face once more, but the monsters are hungry, and there isn't time.

"Come face my monsters with me, Ma." I duck under the bed and drag my mother with me.

PRETEND
BY EMMA E. MURRAY

I am a lizard on the wall, creeping on sticky pads as quickly and quietly as I can. If I'm quiet enough, maybe the snake won't see me.

Skittering down to linoleum, palms and soles flap across the kitchen. The snake is faced away, busy with suds and a casserole dish. I smile, my tongue flicking out and tasting the air. An apple on the counter catches my attention, shiny green and waiting for me. My hand and tongue dart out simultaneously, grabbing it and ducking out of sight. My heart stops. The snake hisses through clenched teeth. She saw me.

"Didn't get enough to eat? Always hungry. Always starving! You fat little fuck, get out of the kitchen." The snake strikes, venom pumping through my veins. I'm caught. I set the apple back on the counter, still pristine, but the meager offering only makes the snake angrier.

"And now you don't want it? Get out of here! I don't want to see your face again tonight."

I go invisible, a gecko's ghost, and make my way up the stairs on the tips of my toes, not a squeak from the steps to give me away.

I am a mouse, quiet nibbles in the corner of the living room. Small hands cupped around a cracker, my eyes dart around, always on the lookout for danger. There's a hawk that circles overhead, but so far, I've stayed out of view. Scurrying across the carpet, I duck out of sight behind the coffee table just as the hawk flies into the room. She has a pile of laundry in her talons, and I let out a warm exhale. She'll be too preoccupied to notice a mouse like me.

Tiny fingers clutch the old board book, the peeling edges soft and worn in my hands. I bring it to my mouth, pretending to gnaw through it, squeaking happily at the find.

"What are you doing? Eating a book? You're not a baby anymore," the hawk snaps out, her words sharper than her beak, puncturing me, tearing deep gashes in my fur and skin.

"I'm just pretending—" I squeak, but her voice rises above mine, ripping me apart.

"Pretending? What are you pretending?" Her voice is tight, caught in a sneer, screeching through my bones, and crushing them to dust. "Pretending to be an idiot who drools all over her things and ruins them?"

"I'm sorry, Momma," I try to say, but the tears bubble over and choke me. The mouse I was lies dead, discarded on the ground, the hawk picking me up and tossing me about, playing with her food. I land on the carpet again and again, limp and gone. But it's the mouse, not me.

"I wish you were never born. You've ruined my life! It's all about you now. Cooking and cleaning and spending every cent on your fucking whims. Can't you see I'm trying to give you everything, and do you even care?"

Finally, the hawk tires of its prey and leaves it strewn in pieces across the carpet.

I am a rabbit, my nose twitching in the morning air, eyes weary of the fog rolling across the lawn. Round and soft on my haunches, I leap out and spread wiry thin, enjoying the shiver of breeze ruffling through my fur. Prancing, bouncing, I make my way to a hill, where I dig my claws into soft dirt and begin building my new warren. I've been foolish, though, let down my guard, and don't see the fox watching me through the kitchen window with narrowed eyes.

The hole grows, but as I make it elbow-deep, something catches me by the collar and yanks me up.

"You don't give a fuck about anything, do you?" the fox growls, and my heart flutters against my ribs, ears rigid, eyes wide. "I just got you this dress, and now look at it. Ruined. Grass stains all over it, and your fingernails, look!" The fox grasps my wrist so tightly it blanches, pulsing white-hot. "Disgusting. Caked with dirt like some sort of animal."

I freeze, my heart hare-fast in my throat.

"I'm sorry, I was playing—" But my whimper is cut off by her howl of rage.

"Oh, don't even start, I *saw*. Bent over like a whore, the whole neighborhood getting an eyeful. I don't want to *ever* see you acting so slutty again. Wear some bicycle shorts under that dress. A fucking little Lolita I'm raising right here."

"But I—"

"Get your ass inside. Wash up and change." Her fox lips curl down into a snarl. "You disgust me."

Burning bright red, I'm a dead rabbit, boiled alive and skinned naked for the neighborhood to point and laugh or pity. The fox marches behind me, a glint of snide cruelty glassy in her eye.

I am a pop star in my heart-shaped glasses and a pink glitter skirt, sparkles dancing under the mall's lights. Momma is smiling, following behind me, and eating her cup of ice cream, yucky pistachio. I finished my chocolate one ages ago. Today is the best day ever, and I bask in my imaginary stardom, feeling gorgeous. I flip my hair over my shoulder and can't stop myself from skipping instead of walking, but halfway across the vast parking lot, I look back, and Momma isn't smiling anymore, so I don't either.

I crawl back into my normal persona and pick at the crumbs of happiness. It can still be a good day.

When we get in the car, Momma slams her door shut, and I sit up straight as a ruler. Every second of the last hour whirs double-speed through my mind's eye, searching desperately for the mistake I must've made. Momma keeps her eyes straight ahead but dabs at them with the edge of her sleeve. I want to tell her I'm sorry for whatever I did, but I don't dare speak first.

We pull up to a red light, and Momma's face snaps toward mine, eyes locked, fuming, and yet hurt.

"You only love me because I buy you things," she says, and before I can argue, she's built an impenetrable wall around herself. She's locked herself in the faraway room in her mind she goes to when she can't handle me anymore.

No matter how much I cry, bang my fists against the car door, beg her to believe me that I love her no matter what, she never has to buy me anything ever again, she doesn't listen. She doesn't even see me anymore. And when we get home, she goes into the house as if I'm not right there next to her, shutting the garage door behind her before I've dragged myself out of the bucket seat.

Her bedroom door is locked. I make her a card, a heart with both of us drawn inside, an apology scrawled beneath, and slip it under the door. She never acknowledges it and doesn't come out until the next evening. Even then, she doesn't speak to me.

I am a girl with a good mommy who loves her and tucks her in every night. A girl who got a cake with sprinkles and new shoes that light up when she walks for her eighth birthday. Not a girl who was forgotten, but one who everyone remembers, admires, adores. Popular and pretty and smart and everything I'm not. I pull my knees to my chest and pretend it's Momma holding me. It makes me feel a little warmer. I can almost smell her perfume in the weave of my shirt, imagine it's her arm pressed to my face, shutting out the night.

The wind whips through my hair as I huddle against the backdoor and shutter my eyes to the shadows of ghouls and spiders prowling over the moon-licked yard, hiding behind trees, waiting for me to fall asleep.

Through the door, I hear the television, and I see myself cuddled under a blanket with Momma, her fingers combing through my hair, gently scratching my head as I drift to sleep.

She whispers that she loves me and I'm the most special girl in the world. I want to tell her I love her, no matter what, but I'm too tired to move my lips. Or am I too cold? It's all right, though. The feeling is passing. The fantasy blossoms, blooming around me in a burst of heat, and I fall into a deep sleep, Momma holding me, rocking me, loving me. It feels more real with every moment, and I don't even mind as the night consumes me because I have Momma.

MOTHER TIDE
BY L. E. DANIELS

Don't lose yourself like I did, she says
as I arrive home, half-drowned sailors in my mouth, a barnacled
hulk my crown.
I spread them, mewling into my palm, asking, *Save them?*
Save yourself, she says. *I should have.* And dashes all to silence.

A tiny girl, cut almost in half, crinkles
and crawls along a shoreline until I take her, wrap her, hold her
close,
but Mother smells the blood.
Stay whole, she tells me, smoothing the girl into rouge.

I fall in love daily, with everything, in secret.
When she finds them in my bed, they're ground to ash before
open windows.
Only Mother tells the truth, she says.
The sea breeze melts their shapes away.

Mother and I skirt round and round;
where she holds, I bend. I lean my currents toward shipwrecks
and lose myself,
dispersed as sailors, undone as girls cleaved—
and full as a lover's lies on a breeze.

Poet's Note: The two main characters could be Demeter and
Persephone or writers like us, but when mothers curtail the
impulses of creative daughters, something emerges regardless—
richer and bolder for its scathing.

NEW AGAIN
BY CHRISTI NOGLE

By the time Lorna was a real kid, by the time she was playing little jokes, getting all excited about cartoons and anxious for bedtime stories, Bonna was forty-five. Not old at all if she'd had a cushy job in the city and a gym membership, but things were different in the country. She surely *felt* old crouching down into the little chair beside Lorna's bed after a day tending animals and garden and trying to hold the old house together, all the time watching the girl with an eagle eye.

She yawned and turned to riffle through storybooks. "What do you want to hear tonight, sweetie?"

"I want to hear about Stacie," said Lorna.

"Again?" said Bonna, but she wasn't surprised—or displeased, really. She had never hidden this story from the girl, but it was only recently that Lorna had started wanting to know more than the barest outlines: *You had a sister once, before you were born. She's gone forever.*

Tonight, Bonna talked about herself and Stacie and Stacie's dad, her first husband Von—how they'd been so young and so new to country life that in the evenings, instead of television, they'd take walks along the looping roads and stop to say hi to the neighbors. As she spoke, the scenery came to her, the way the light hit the fields, the little creek—all of it still outside if she cared to look.

The hollowed-out house across the fields stayed far from her mind as though it had never existed.

And Bonna laughed to remember: When they walked later in the summer and into fall, they'd come home with more vegetables than she could carry. The neighbors all brightened to see them. All three of them had been so young. All was freedom and smiles.

"Did Stacie walk all the way?" asked Lorna, her eyes wide but false, as though she knew the answer.

"Oh, no, *he* would carry her when she got tired," Bonna said.

Stacie had also ridden a Shetland pony when she was a little older, but she couldn't bear to say so to this girl who'd never had a pony. In the earliest days, Von had carried her. Bonna thought of his face so like Lorna's, which was so like Stacie's. She could see the other girl, just exactly like this one, her arms around Von's neck, body bobbing against his chest, that face— this face—blissful in the sunset light.

Lorna yawned, which made her mother yawn again.

"We better get some rest," said Bonna. Her leg asleep, she moved off the bed with a wince.

"*Who* carried her?" asked Lorna, and when her mother did not answer, she said, "It was Daddy. I remember."

A tear sneaked down the side of Bonna's face. "Yes," she said, though Lorna had never before called that distant man Daddy and had no real memories of him.

Bonna flicked off the lamp and pulled the covers around her girl. Lorna said something too quiet to make out.

Bonna left the room and turned out all the lights downstairs. She would never be brave again, but Lorna was brave enough to like the dark. She bolted the locks high up on the front and back doors, checked the windows, and climbed up to her bedroom. All the time, she wondered what the girl had asked.

Why is Stacie gone forever? Was that what she had asked, or was it something else—*Is she* really *gone forever?* Or maybe it hadn't been a question at all.

Lorna's first day of kindergarten came two weeks after the start of school. She'd been too sick the first week, raving in a fever. Maybe she would have been all right the next week, but Bonna worried. She wanted to be safe. That's why there'd never been a pony for this girl. That's why there'd been strict rules about staying in sight, staying in bed at night, all of that.

It was a good thing school was starting. That meant Bonna could be working soon. She needed to work, get out in the world a little.

Bonna stood holding Lorna's hand, waiting for the bus, looking across the fields to the hollowed-out house. No sign of its walls after all these years, nothing but an open basement in the middle of a field. A chain link fence stood around it ever since what had happened to Stacie.

Lorna had cried a lot while she was sick. "I fell. I hurt so bad," she had called up from the depths of her fever. "I just wanted to be new again. I wasn't Lorna yet."

She'd been raving, agitated, and Bonna hadn't caught whatever bug it was, but she had caught the delusion, or maybe it was only a fantasy. She had been asking questions, falling into the fantasy right along with her daughter.

Where did you fall? What was hurt? What was your name, then, if it wasn't Lorna?

(Was it Stacie? Could it be?)

What were you doing out there all alone? If you wanted to go walking, why didn't you wake Daddy and me? We'd have gone with you.

But it's all right now—you're new. You're perfect.

Humoring her. That's all it had been.

Now, the air felt cool on their faces, and the skies said summer was not all the way done. Bonna stood straight, held Lorna's hand. They watched the bus coming from a long way off and spoke of how bright the future would be.

Stacie's school clothes were still new in tags for Lorna, but maybe they weren't in style anymore. Bonna didn't think of that until much later. Could it be, all the way out here, that having out-of-date clothes led to what happened? Would that have been enough to mark Lorna as different, to make the other children start pecking at her?

Not that the pecking came right away. There were always precursors.

Once, Bonna's father had brought home one of those fancy chickens with the powderpuff heads. When they sat it in with the other chickens, all seemed well, but that one kept getting slower and weaker. Bonna didn't think they went at its head right away; it was more that they wouldn't let it eat, and then when it got weak enough, they started the pecking. The powderpuff head turned to a brown mop, and then the feathers started falling out until one day, the pretty little chicken was all used up and dead there in the dooryard.

So, with Lorna: There were all the small slights that made her weak, and then after the weakness came the pecking. Bullying seemed an insufficient term to cover the range of what happened to Lorna in those first few years of school. It was like the entire world yearned to destroy her sweet girl.

Maybe the clothes were to blame, or maybe it was because Bonna had been overprotective, or maybe it was because she couldn't keep Von from running away when Lorna was tiny. Usually, Bonna found a way to blame herself, but sometimes she blamed the children and, by extension, this place. Would everything have been different if she'd followed Von back to the city after Stacie died? Wouldn't the world around Lorna have been less insular, more open to variation?

Other times, secretly, Bonna thought that Lorna brought it all on herself. Not by how she acted but because of what she was. Something unnatural (Newer than she ought to have been? Older than she really was?). But these were secret thoughts and hidden.

Regardless of the cause, from that moment the school bus door opened (and the driver, remembering what had happened years before, looked on Bonna with pity), from that moment letting go of her mother's hand, Lorna was ... distressed.

By fourth grade, fifth grade, it reached a peak. After a bad day at school, Lorna would be hyperventilating, grasping wildly for things that might hurt her. Her mother held her arms, held her wrists, and said *It's going to be okay*. Bonna wasn't so good, herself, by then.

Lorna put a hand to Bonna's stomach and said, *pleaded*, "I want to be new again." Bonna couldn't admit it to herself afterward, but right at that moment, she knew exactly what her daughter meant and thought there might be just enough time, still, to do it. Find Von, wherever he'd gone, go desperate into his arms. Make her girl again. Make her new.

Like you did for me the last time after I died out in the field.

But there were years between. You couldn't have, and even if—

Humoring her? No, Bonna couldn't say that was what she was doing anymore.

There was something about having Lorna so close, so desperate, their hearts beating hard. In Lorna's little pink bedroom, this was. It had never been redecorated, not since she was a baby. Longer: not since she was Stacie. And so Bonna *entertained* the idea. With her hand on the belly, Lorna said wordlessly that they both knew.

Bonna nodded, and Lorna flinched away. Her eyes went wide, and then she closed them and backed out of the room.

Bonna hadn't fought against the truth, and maybe that's what had finally healed things. Lorna saw her mother was willing and that she would need to be the one to back away from the monstrous idea, and so she did.

Certainly, after this incident, Lorna changed. She forced herself to be calmer, to be healthy, or if she could not do that much, she at least pretended. The bond between them weakened—as it needed to, as it *had to*—and the girl began to focus outward, toward friends, toward the future.

On the lawn that humid day Lorna graduated from high school, Bonna studied the triangle made by the girl, herself, and

Von, who had flown in with his new wife and the twins. Bonna herself was flanked by friends from work. She watched Lorna, the moment the hats had been tossed, put her arms around her two best friends. The boyfriend, Steven, came up behind Lorna and swept her off her feet. Bonna smiled, and the tears came down hard. Her friends squeezed her hands.

The hollowed-out house was finally replaced with a tall white one with columns, black shutters. Bonna stood staring at the house sometimes before she checked her mailbox. A woman Lorna's age lived there now with a little boy and a toddler, a sheepdog, and a delicate, handsome man. They all sat out on the porch in the evenings. People would come by to visit, but the family never walked the roads in the evening, which Bonna found endlessly sad.

Bonna's life was happy, though. She enjoyed time with friends, even more so after retiring. She liked the short, polite phone calls with her daughter. Lorna was happy, too. She said she was.

But a shiver started when the girl said something dismissive about her husband. Steven was a good guy, Bonna had never doubted that. But there it was again, the next time they talked. Nothing much, just *Oh, Steven wouldn't understand. You know how he is.* Not just dismissive but resentful, snide. She heard pain and distress in her daughter's voice and dreaded the day when Lorna would run away back home.

That day came in a blink. Lorna was more controlled than in girlhood, but still, she wept and went blank. She said mad things. *Don't act like you don't know. There's something wrong with me. I just want* ... and then nothing about what she wanted. She wouldn't say it, and Bonna felt she'd do anything to keep Lorna from saying it. Bonna's life now had that edge back to it, like walking on eggshells—or skipping along the edge of a chasm.

"I just want to be new," Lorna finally said a week in. This time, she looked not at Bonna but out across the fields to the tall white house and the woman playing in its yard with her sweet little boys and her big, sloppy dog.

Electric pain pulsed between Bonna's eyebrows. She gasped at the sensation. "No," she said in horror. "You wouldn't be you anymore."

Lorna nodded and looked at her phone. She was going to call Steven. She was going to try to do it herself this time.

Over salad that night, Bonna said, "People think youth is the best part of life, Lorna, but that isn't true. I'm happier now than I ever was, now that I'm old. I love my friends."

And *my thoughts are not so strange as they once were,* but was that true? She still thought of parading around the roads, leading the little pony.

Bubbles. Stacie had named him herself.

Lorna's phone dinged. She said, "He'll be here in three or four hours. You'll be in bed by then."

Bonna was in bed by then, feeling numb. Steven's headlights lit the trees outside her window, a slow pattern of leaves swept across her room, and then there was nothing. She couldn't hear them moving in the pink bedroom below. Maybe they only sat in the kitchen talking.

He was gone in the morning, anyway. He'd served his purpose.

Bonna's head couldn't clear. She was still caught in the wonderings of the night before. The image of Lorna's belly stretched impossibly taut, with two navels in it. The image of Lorna turning inside out in labor, her own body disappearing, sucking into itself. Nothing like that would happen, surely.

Bonna regretted that she rarely did anything anymore. With Lorna home, the friends had all grown distant. She wondered whether they wanted to give the two time alone or because, at the heart of things, Lorna was still inexpressibly repellant to people.

But Lorna seemed to be working on herself. She brought the groceries home and checked the mail. She crossed the fields and lingered, talking to the neighbor woman, Tiffy. (Oh, how could she go near that house?) The two of them, consciously or not, put hands to their still-flat bellies. Lorna painted green over the pink and set to work on a mural of tigers and leaves. She brought home a sheepdog puppy from that house but then returned it within a week. Too much mess.

Lorna said, "What we really need to look for is a pony. I'll pick up a *Thrifty Nickel* next time I go."

Would the baby *be* Lorna? And then, if so, what could that mean? Would the mother-body be a blank then? Soulless. Walking around changing diapers without a soul anymore.

No. Bonna would be the one changing diapers. She knew that. No matter what else happened, she would still be the mother.

I *want to be new*, she thought absently.

Lorna was better than she had ever been before. She went to her appointments, took her vitamins. She was polite and personable in town, which she'd never been, even in the best days of high school. When her doctor suggested more exercise, she took to walking the country roads and brought back vegetable offerings. She did much credit card spending in town.

"I always wanted one of these," she would say, setting the motion lamp or the curly teddy bear or whatever new thing into her room.

"You didn't like the pink?" Bonna would say at the start. "Didn't you love the books we had there?" As the changes came together, she could see it would be much finer than the room she'd made for Lorna. It made her disappointed, ashamed, and hopeful. Maybe this time, her daughter's life would feel better to her.

As Lorna swelled, their talks became quite open, morbid, and fantastical.

"Do you think the baby will have Steven's hair?" Bonna said absently.

Lorna waited a long time before answering. "I think I'll be me again, just as I am."

"But how could that be?"

"I think he provided something, but not what a father usually does. Let's say he provided a spark for a … parthenogenesis."

And that felt true. Were Lorna and Stacie identical? Bonna couldn't say. They'd been so many years apart. They'd had no birthmarks, never been fingerprinted.

"There was a footprint on the birth certificate," Lorna said, but did footprints identify someone like a fingerprint did? They located Stacie's in a stack of old papers by the freezer but couldn't find Lorna's for comparison.

"Have you thought of names?" Steven texted. He'd finally found out and was expecting to be involved.

"Her name is Stacie," Lorna texted back.

"And what will happen to you?" Bonna said, but Lorna never answered.

The labor wasn't easy, and Bonna was a wreck all the time they were at the hospital. She thought this was why Lorna had never answered her question: she'd expected to die, to pass into the baby.

Steven came. He was kinder than anyone could have been under the circumstances. Bonna couldn't say whether she hoped or feared a reconciliation. If the baby were to go home with him—or even if Lorna lived and the two of them went home with him—wouldn't that be for the best? And yet she *wanted* the baby. She wanted Stacie, new again, so mother and baby both had to live.

Steven would meet what he thought was his baby. He might follow them home and help them get settled, but then he would return to his little rowhouse and his job. The mother and grandmother would carry Stacie on walks around the neighborhood, up until she was old enough to ride on her Shetland pony. It couldn't be otherwise.

Baby Stacie was a surprise, though. She was born with a dark stain on her shoulder and quite a lot of hair, unlike the first Stacie and unlike Lorna.

Lorna stroked the hair and looked at Bonna, who could not read her expression.

"She's probably just a little later than you were," Bonna said when Steven wasn't in the room.

Lorna sighed. She'd been awfully vague since the delivery, uttering only the barest yes or no to the questions nurses asked. Usually yes. Yes, she was comfortable; yes, she could eat; yes, she wanted to hold the baby.

All was more or less as Bonna expected. Steven went home at the end of the next week, leaving her the only one to fetch things. Lorna and the baby lay in their narrow bed in their room decorated with tigers and ferns. Lorna passed the baby to Bonna for cleaning and, rarely at first but more each day, she lay her in the bassinet and sat back with a long sigh. It was rare she said anything other than yes or thank you.

Bonna tried to spark conversation—tried to get Lorna excited about the days to come, when they would walk in the neighborhood and later, when they would lead Stacie's little pony again. She grew sentimental, even maudlin. They would lead her pony, and this time, Stacie would grow strong and fearless even as they kept her safe. Later, she would ride the pony by herself and eventually get a tall Paint or an Appaloosa—"Which do you think, Lorna?"

Lorna said, "Yes."

All would be well. This Stacie would go to kindergarten in brand-new clothes, and with the two of them to mother her, her hair would always be clean and combed. She would bring friends home to her lovely, clean room to play. Anything that happened at school, they would talk through. They could even move if that were for the best.

"Do you think we might want to go somewhere larger? Better schools, of course, and more diverse people for her to meet. More places to see. I always wondered," Bonna said.

Lorna only said, "Yes." She sighed and turned toward the wall.

More and more frantic, Bonna grew, talking all alone.

The little neighbor woman Tiffy was presumably in bed with her own newcomer. Bonna saw her pretty husband going in and out with the boys and the dog. Soon, though, Tiffy came out again. Her figure had snapped back right away, unlike Lorna's. She had not lost her bouncy way of moving, though now a huge baby was strapped to her front. She played with the dog and the boys again, and one day, she came out alone with just the bundle, walking briskly across the fields.

Bonna saw her coming and waited outside the door, greeted her, and admired the baby boy, who was as plump as that sheepdog puppy had been.

She leaned back into the house, called, "Lorna, are you up for company?"

"Yes," Lorna called weakly.

Bonna wished that just that once, she could have said no. It wasn't only that it hurt to see them together, Tiffy so strong and lively compared to Lorna, her baby so fat and happy compared to Stacie. It also bothered Bonna that when she left them and went into the kitchen, she heard Tiffy's long, excited questions and the short spaces of Lorna's answers. Her yesses.

Bonna tried to wash dishes but couldn't help herself; she went back toward the room.

Tiffy sat in the chair beside the bed with her arm around Lorna, who cried silently, eyes closed. When Tiffy looked up at Bonna, her expression held worry, blame, and something more. It stopped Bonna, sent her back a few steps. She pressed herself against the wall.

"My sister had trouble like this," said Tiffy.

Lorna said, "Yes," and then let out a shuddering sound as though she were very cold.

"We just need to get you some help, is all. You'll be right as rain," said Tiffy.

There was a long empty silence, and then Lorna said, "I was so far back inside. Whenever I wanted anything, it was so terrible, and so I just always agreed. After a while, I always just thought *yes*. I don't even know what else to say anymore. I—" and she fell into choking sobs.

"Agreed with whom?" said Tiffy. Something about *whom* angered Bonna. What kind of person talked that way?

"Are you talking about your mother?" Tiffy said, and there was silence. Bonna could not see if Lorna nodded or shook her head.

Bonna moved quietly out of the hall and into the kitchen. She sat at the table, closed her eyes, and wept. The new baby was not Stacie at all, which meant that Lorna had never been Stacie either.

All had been delusion, and whose delusion had it been? Had Lorna started it, or had she? Bonna must have told the girl stories she didn't remember telling, made interpretations that went too far, and worked on suppositions and hopes (hopes, most of all).

She could not believe or even comprehend what Lorna was struggling to tell Tiffy just now: that there *was* a second daughter who had until she gave birth a few weeks ago, never controlled her own body or even her mind. That the child in the bassinet was and always had been a monster, a parasite. That was unthinkable, and so Bonna believed that it had only been her and Lorna all these years.

And she had warped Lorna into something inhuman.

The baby, though, the small and quiet new baby with Steven's hair and eyes, what did she deserve? To go with her father. There was no other answer.

And so, through the ordeal of the next half hour walking Tiffy out of the house and back across the fields, hearing her recommendations for supplements and therapies and things that could bring on joy, deflecting the hints of accusation, Bonna had to keep very clear in her mind what to do. She had to avoid being swayed from her course. It would be the hardest thing she ever did, the only thing that mattered.

MOTHER KNOWS BEST

BY CRYSTAL SIDELL

Mother mixes pretty cocktails–
amber, scintillant blue, slime green.

> Drink up!
>> Drink up!
> Don't spill a drop!

Some taste sweet, some bitter.

But always after: pricking needles,
lights in my eyes, the stethoscope
pressed to my chest–

the doctor measuring the drawings
of my unsteady breaths.

Mother floats across the carpet,
humming bright tunes with each advance.

> Drink up!
>> Drink up!
> Swallow every drop!

How the sour hurts my stomach.

Too-sharp needles, too-bright lights. Again
the cold stethoscope pressed to my chest–
the rattling of my labored breaths.

                          What did you eat?
                    What did you drink?
          Did you swallow a pill?
                    Peel paint off the walls?

Clinging to my toy penguin, I shake
my head on the hospital pillow.

          I only take what Mother gives me–

even if it churns my stomach,
even if it burns my chest.

Because Mother loves me. Yes, she does.
And Mother always knows what's best.

THE TIRED MOM SMOOTHIE
BY BROOKE MACKENZIE

She is so sweet. You could just eat her up: those rosy little toddler cheeks, those strawberry-blond ringlets, the staccato starbursts of her laughter as you play your little games together. You find yourself feeling so very grateful to have a daughter. And you find yourself feeling so very tired.

Your days are tethered to the smooth surface of your routine: feed her oatmeal, drop her off at preschool, kiss your husband before he leaves for the office, and then begin the swayback drudgery of your chores (dishes, fabric softener, groceries, meal prep, straightening up, folding, dishes, organizing, vacuuming, the yawning creak of closing full drawers, taking out the trash, and somehow even more dishes). They constitute the rhythm of your life, these tasks that define your minutes. They are the boxes that fill your planner, and when you look in the mirror, it's as if your skin has been replaced by those words. You are just a fleshy to-do list.

Sometimes you find one of your daughter's stray socks or her petal pink blankie balled up in the corner, and you pick it up, and smell it, and miss her. Not just miss her, but a deep ache radiates through your muscles as your arms feel her absence. And then you remember that it is because of her that you spend your time this way, and it's why you've taken the part of you that used to create tapestries of music with the spinnerets of your fingers and buried it underneath the slate gray labors of motherhood.

You break the day's monotony by scrolling through TikTok in your few spare moments, which is how you first heard of the Tired Mom Smoothie that is supposed to revolutionize your life and energy levels and burn away the tender pockets of leftover pregnancy fat that just won't go away. You order the smoothie. One day, after returning home from the preschool drop-off and dry cleaner drop-off, and grocery pick-up, a little brown package is sitting by your door, covered in words screaming, WELCOME TO THE NEW AND IMPROVED YOU, MAMA! Inside the package, you find several bags of powder that looks and smells like baby formula, with a handwritten note that simply says, 100% ORGANIC INGREDIENTS, MIX WELL WITH ONE CUP OF WATER. You shrug and figure that if it's good enough for the TikTokers, it's good enough for you. So, you mix it well and drink it down, and it has a pleasant vanilla flavor.

Preschool pick-up is like feeding time at the zoo with the noises and shrieking and smells—that aroma of bleach tainted with dirty diapers. Your daughter runs to you, adds her own bellow of "MOMMY!" to the din, and hugs you around your knees. Your heart is a plucked string, and it shakes loose all these endorphins, and you can't believe that the halcyon light of your love is simply made up of chemicals from your brain. You hug her, feel her cheek bow under your lips as you kiss her, and whisk her away to the car seat that always seems like a torture device.

At home, you will yourself to sprout another pair of hands. Your husband retreats to his video games, citing a long day at work, while you chop and sauté and peel and scrub and manage the Lego pile and hand her the markers and help her go potty and sop up the meltdowns like a ragged, human mop. The meltdowns churn your eardrums into a kind of butter that makes your thoughts greasy. She spends much of the evening facedown in her own verbal pile of NO!!, and it makes you ineffably exhausted. Your husband yells his commentary from the other room. But then, the food is on the table, everyone is in a seat, and you realize that you haven't eaten since drinking the Tired Mom Smoothie. You haven't even been hungry. You choke down a few bites of your dinner, but then your stomach roils uncomfortably, so you pack it up, put it in the fridge, and feel victorious over your appetite. You put a hand on your belly, bidding it adieu, as it will not be long for this world.

Then it's bath time and story time and wrestling into the nighttime pull-ups and the pre-bed screaming and the pleading, and then finally, finally she falls asleep, and you prepare to enjoy the thirty-minute window of relaxation time that you experience nightly before you succumb to sleep. Except, tonight, you don't want to sleep. No, you don't *need* to sleep. You feel suddenly nocturnal, so you give into this newfound surge of nighttime energy and stay awake doing more tasks. You wait to get hungry, you wait to get tired, but somehow, you don't do either.

The next morning, you make yourself another smoothie (this time, it seems as though the flavor has changed … it's how you imagine damp grass would taste, and it is still somehow delicious) and glide through the morning routine. This afternoon, after the morning chores are done, you meet up with a group of other mom friends for your standing weekly date. You all order lavender lattes, sit in your usual sunny corner around a too-small table, and talk in too-loud voices about your husbands and children, in-laws, and neighbors, and everyone else's updates and interests and gossip and happenings. No one talks about their interests or passions or hobbies or self-care routines because you are all empty, like the cups you will eventually leave behind on the table.

Today, as you listen intently to your friends, you realize you are finally feeling hungry. But it's not a kind of hunger you've ever felt before. It's not the kind of hunger from skipping one, two, or three meals. It's a deeper, more primal hunger. One woman talks about her son's baseball, swimming, and skiing; the hunger makes your skin itch. You start scratching yourself, hoping no one will notice, but then you can't stop your fingernails from raking over your flesh, providing relief, and it makes a dry scraping sound, and soon everyone is staring.

"Hey, hon, are you okay? Do you need some lotion?"

You nod and accept the lotion and notice that when you stick out your tongue to wet your lips, you can actually taste the flavor of that cloying floral lotion in the air. You do it again and notice that you can taste your latte without even having to drink it. You can taste the post-yoga sweat on the neck of the woman next to you. And as you begin to taste these things around you, the hunger becomes even more overwhelming, but you don't want to eat anything in that coffee shop. You don't quite know what you want to eat. Your skin starts to itch again, and then finally, you excuse yourself because your senses are clanging like a hundred dinner bells, and you just need to get to the confined space of your car.

Before buckling your seatbelt, you examine your skin and see that the texture looks different—dry and smooth at the same time. Are those *scales*? You make a mental note to call your dermatologist because clearly your eczema is back. As you look out the windshield on your drive home, you notice your vision has changed. You can suddenly see more shades and hues than usual, which is especially surprising since, recently, it appears as though your eyes have aged, and everything you see is dull and muted. You can almost feel your lenses changing shape as you shift your focus to different objects—some near, some far—and you take in everything in more detail than you ever thought possible. Your eyes are porous sponges; images and colors saturate them, filling you with a torrent of energy, of liquid life. You decide this must be what the smoothie meant by the new and improved you.

You steer the car toward home and the steady afternoon of tasks ahead of you. But, instead of doing them, you find yourself bounding up the stairs to the attic where you stored your baby grand piano. You previously told yourself that it's only up there temporarily, that toddlers and pianos are a headache-inducing combination, that you didn't want her sticky fingers to stain your keys while she pounded them into oblivion. But you know it isn't temporary, that your music has been relegated to your own internal dusty attic.

Today, however, some other instinct overrides your decision-making skills. You need the music to camouflage you from the predatory nature of your days—days that feast on your time, energy, and dreams. And so, you play. And play and play and play. You play until you think the notes might crack the roof. You play until you have created a shelter of sound in which to hide away. You play like a frantic, wild animal racing toward its own survival. The itching in your arms has stopped, and you see that they are, in fact, covered in scales, each one a little peach teardrop. You are not surprised. This feels right. And you rub them, in awe of how impossibly smooth they are, the way your muscles undulate under them, and you realize that for the first time in a long time, you feel so very awake. The new and improved you.

The hunger comes back and almost bowls you over, and now it's time for preschool pick-up. You can taste the children in the air. Your tongue flicks in and out, wetting your lips, and you can taste the musky, sweaty, piss-soaked flavor of them all.

"MOMMY!" She runs to you and hugs your kneecaps and tastes like paint and clay and cheese. You secure her into her car seat harness, tightening it until she cannot move.

The two of you drive off, and you taste the air that is filled with her, and it is delicious and juicy, like a ripe little plum. She *is* a ripe little plum. Her laughter is sugar water coating the air like a glaze. Her cheeks produce a scent that makes your innards liquefy in digestive juices, wanting to replenish the energy you have expended since becoming a mother. You have to pull the car over because the hunger is too strong. Your tongue flicks in and out, your lenses shift to take in more color, and you think your jaw is slowly loosening, dislocating, opening.

She is so sweet. You could just eat her up.

YOUR MOTHER'S LOVE
IS AN APOCALYPSE
BY GWENDOLYN KISTE

It's Thursday morning when they call to tell you your mother is trying to destroy the world again.

"We thought she was still dormant," they whisper on the other end, as though they're afraid she'll hear them. What they don't seem to understand is she can hear you no matter where you are.

You're still in bed, the sun peeking in the window, the pale sheets tangled up around you. You want to hang up the phone. You want to tell them to leave you alone, that your mother is not and has never been your responsibility.

"I'll be there by tonight," you say instead.

"Thank you, Selena," they say, and the line goes dead.

You're never quite sure who it is that calls you. The sniveling mayor of your old hometown, perhaps, or a county commissioner. It's not the feds, that's for sure. Your town does its best to keep your mother a secret. She might want to destroy the whole world, but she'll have to start with her own flea-speck city, and as far as the locals are concerned, that's never going to happen. They've even passed an ordinance against your mother for all the good it did them.

As you toss your phone on the nightstand, a shadow dances across your face, and with your heart tight in your chest, you jolt toward it.

But it's only Mindy standing in the doorway, still wearing your shirt from last night.

"It's your mom again, isn't it?" she asks, and you nod, turning away from her, not wanting her to see the fear flashing in your eyes.

Not that it makes any difference. Your wife knows you well enough to know when you're afraid. She also knows there's no point in arguing with you once you've made up your mind. Without a word, she packs you a lunch like you're a schoolgirl heading off on a field trip. Sliced apples and a peanut butter and jelly sandwich cut into squares. But even as she hands you the brown paper bag on your way out the front door, that doesn't mean she wants you to leave.

"You don't have to do this," she says, and you wish that were true.

"I love you," you say and kiss her goodbye.

The state highway that leads back to your hometown is long and winding, and you could drive it with your eyes closed. This is the third time your mother's done this, and part of you fears this could be it. This could be the end.

Your mother, the ultimate cosmic horror. You'd like to say you never saw this coming, but let's face it: you're the one person in the world who knew this was a possibility. That's because you're the only person who saw what your mother was really like. The flashes of rage, sharp as daggers. The empty place in her heart where remorse should be. She had a cruel streak wider than the Mississippi, and nobody realized it but you.

Or rather, they didn't want to realize it. The whole town did their best to ignore what she was becoming. And to ignore your pleas for help.

"Selena's such an impossible girl," everyone said about you because it was easier to blame you than believe you.

It's nearly midnight when you pass the county line. Even before you can see your hometown, you can feel it. The rumble deep within the earth. The poisonous lullaby of your mother.

As you drive through the vacant streets, you gaze up at all the houses. And the houses gaze back at you. The townspeople are hiding inside, peeking out from behind the blinds, their fingers clenched around tattered curtains.

On a corner at the edge of town, you press hard on the brake, the engine bucking beneath you, as you stare up at the two-story brick house with the faded mint green shutters. Your childhood home. There are no lights on inside, but that doesn't mean it's vacant. When you've returned in the past, you tried again and again to get inside, but all the windows and doors were locked. A few of the local men did their best to help you, turning a fallen telephone pole into a battering ram, but the house wouldn't budge.

Your mother apparently did not want visitors.

You park downtown beneath the courthouse clocktower and have the sandwich and apple slices Mindy packed for you. It could be hours before you'll have another decent meal. It could be days.

Then you meet the others at the town square as you always do. There's usually a crowd of a couple dozen people, but tonight, it's just the mayor and a few of his assistants.

"Thank you for coming," they say, but they look right past you, never seeing you, only seeing what you can do for them. In this town, some things never change.

Your mother, however, has changed enough for all of you. You're standing next to a crevice she's cracked open in the pavement. Your hands clasped in front of you, you tiptoe toward it and sneak a glance inside. There's nothing but gray darkness yawning within.

"Have you seen her?" you ask the others, but they all shake their heads.

"Not lately," they say. It's as if she's become mist, merging with the atmosphere, everything and nothing at the same time.

The only thing you ever witness from her is the desolation in her wake. And there's plenty of that. All the buildings in the business district have been split down the middle of their stone foundations, and there's hellfire coming from the double doors of the traffic court where your mother lost her license three times over the years. Hit and run, DUI. Everyone knew something was wrong, but other than issuing a quick citation, they just looked the other way.

"You'll be all right," they told you, back when you were so small that your mother could practically crush you with a single look. They didn't care about the curling iron burns on your forehead or the quiet look of fear in your eyes. All that mattered was keeping things quiet. What they didn't understand was that your mother wouldn't be quieted for long.

With your head down, you kept wondering if things would ever get better. Because even after you graduated high school and went off to college and did all the things expected of you, it never really mattered. Your whole future still felt as hazy and empty as your past.

Then, all at once, everything changed. It was at a rooftop Halloween party, the October clouds gone gray in the sky when you met Mindy. You were a grad school dropout then, eagerly headed toward being a life dropout, too. She was dressed as a skeleton in a tight black bodysuit, and you were arrayed in the getup of a gravedigger, shovel and all.

"We look like we belong together," Mindy said, her skin sweet-scented like lavender and vanilla. She asked you to dance even though there was no music, and you couldn't help but tell her yes.

"You don't want me," you said the next morning, still naked in her bed. "You don't know what I come from."

But she only smiled, running her fingers softly through your hair. "You're more than your past," she said, and back then, you wanted to believe that.

Mindy was nothing like the people you grew up with. Whenever you told her about what happened to you—the way the ground would tremble at your mother's fury, how her eyes went black with rage and her hands curled into ugly fists and time would stop at her command—Mindy always believed you.

"You're safe now," she'd say, her hand entwined with yours, the two of you instantly inseparable. Road trips and art openings and late-night dinners cooked barefoot together. It was everything you'd ever hoped your life could be.

This was real. This would last. That was what you promised yourself when you got down on one knee at your favorite Italian restaurant and asked her to marry you. At that moment, it was all so traditional you almost had to laugh.

Of course, your mother hated Mindy, refused to even acknowledge her. She told you over and over how you should have ended up with your college boyfriend.

"Why couldn't you marry Grant?" she asked. "I liked him."

You just shrugged. "I liked him too for a while," you said because it was true. He wasn't the worst, and in fact, he was better than the other men who left constellations of bruises up and down your arms. With him, it was love until it wasn't, the same way so many relationships end. You and Grant didn't even part on bad terms. Every December, you exchange Christmas cards, and last year, you and Mindy went to his wedding at a vineyard upstate. You bought him and his new bride a Cuisinart food processor off their registry at Bed Bath and Beyond. A perfectly banal end to a perfectly banal partnership.

Except you didn't want a banal life. You wanted something better than what you came from. Only that wasn't what your mother wanted for you. She wanted a daughter she could be proud of. And you were anything but that.

The last conversation you ever had with her was about your own wedding and how she wouldn't be there.

"You were always so difficult," your mother said, as if marrying the woman you love was just another of your so-called temper tantrums.

But you're not the one with all the rages. The mayor creeps alongside you as you inspect the latest round of destruction. It's even worse than you expected. A whole row of houses on the West Side pulverized into dust. You shiver, not wanting to ask if there were still people inside when your mother's frenzy flattened the street.

"We hoped she would stop this eventually," the mayor whispers, but you just scoff because if he knew her even half as well as you did, he'd know that she's never going to stop.

It was during your honeymoon that your mother first threatened to shatter the world. You were two thousand miles away in Vegas when a chasm split open in the middle of Main Street, and everyone nearby heard something skittering within. That was when you got the first call from the unknown voice begging you to come back. To come home.

You sat on the edge of your wedding bed, the satin sheets crinkled around you, your head in your hands.

"Please stay," Mindy whispered, her dark hair falling over her eyes.

"I have to go," you said, even though you didn't know why.

That first time, you stayed in town for a week, cleaning up the mess your mother made. Broken buildings, broken lives. The ground didn't stop shaking until Sunday. The day your honeymoon was due to end.

"You always get what you want, don't you?" you asked your mother before you climbed back into your rental car and drove the six hours back to your apartment. Mindy had taken a plane ride home alone, her eyes limned red. She never complained. She only held you close once you were together.

"Don't leave me again," your wife whispered to you, but you said nothing in return. You didn't want to make a promise you knew you couldn't keep.

Now, here you are, right where you started. A tentacle slithers up from beneath the earth and wraps around your ankle. With a scowl, you kick it away.

The mayor and his underlings excuse themselves to assist a family cowering in an alleyway. They lost their home with the rest, the remainder of their lives stuffed into a stained duffel bag.

"Is that the daughter?" someone whispers, and you hear the mayor gossiping about you as you pass.

You try not to listen. You've got to find your mother. Or at least you've got to find a way to stop her. There's a row of oak trees uprooted on Third Street and a lightning storm that's only hitting the park. You watch the bright, jagged flashes in the night sky like it's a fireworks show on the Fourth of July. Then you keep going.

"Mom?" Your voice echoes into the empty night. "Where are you?"

The stench of sulfur and regret linger in the air, but nobody in this town answers you. Instead, someone far away is calling you. In your pocket, the phone rings, and even without glancing down at the number, you know it's Mindy.

"How are you?" she asks, her voice ragged. You can tell she's been crying ever since you left.

"I'm fine," you say, though you both know it's a lie. There's nothing fine about fixing your mother's mistakes.

"You don't need to stay there," Mindy says, static crackling between you. "She isn't your responsibility."

"I love you," you say and hang up the phone.

The night pushes in closer around you. No matter where you go, your hometown is always waiting for you, nestled in the Appalachian Mountains, mist obscuring the horizon. You sometimes wonder what kind of person you might have been if you hadn't ended up here with a mother like her. Would you be happier? Would you feel free? At the very least, you wouldn't be in the one place you promised yourself you would escape.

The place that helped to create the horror that is your mother.

You're not sure what she even looks like anymore. The last time you were home was almost three years ago, and you didn't see your mother face to face. You only saw what she did to this town. That was the second time your mother did her best to destroy the world, and she almost succeeded. You stayed for over a month, calling out to the wind, to nothing at all, desperate to stop her or maybe even slow her down, all the while this place leeching into you like a cancer. But with the tremble in the earth waning at last, that seemed to appease your mother.

It didn't appease the rest of the world, however. By the time you returned to your real life, you'd lost your job at the accounting firm, and Mindy was already starting to pack up the house.

"I thought you were gone for good," she said. "I thought your mother had finally won."

"Not yet," you whispered, though you couldn't help but wonder how much longer until that would be true.

"Why do you do it?" Mindy asked you that night. "Why do you go back there?"

You wouldn't look at her. "Because nobody else can."

If you don't help the town, then everything will crumble.

You're two blocks away from home when you see someone up ahead in a front yard. It's a little girl in pigtails, no older than eight or nine, and she's jump-roping as if it isn't past midnight, as if it isn't the end of the world. As you get closer, she grins at you, a cavern where her two front teeth should be.

You seize up at the edge of her lawn. "You shouldn't be out here."

"Neither should you," the little girl says, and she's not wrong.

Even though you don't invite her, the little girl walks with you for a while. "My parents talk about you sometimes," she says as the two of you approach your old house.

"Do they?" you ask absently.

"They say everybody knows this is your fault." The little girl chews her bottom lip. "If you hadn't made her angry—"

"Then what?" you ask, your voice cold as stone. Cold as the dead. "What would have happened if I'd done what my mother told me to?"

The little girl shrugs. "I don't know. It's just what the adults say."

You exhale a thin sigh. "Adults don't know everything."

A tiny crystalline laugh. "They sure don't."

You linger on the street in front of your home, gazing up at this place that made you. The same place that all but destroyed you. It's a truth no one will acknowledge: there's no room in the world for unloved daughters. You're just supposed to smile and give thanks for every crumb of make-believe affection you get.

"She cares about you in her own way," the others would say, and you suppose if destruction is a form of affection, then your mother is chockful of it.

But then again, that's the problem. Your mother honestly believes she loves you. She believes real love hurts sometimes.

"You're my baby," she would say to you, her arms wrapped around you so tight you couldn't breathe. "You're mine, you're mine, you're mine."

As you take a step forward, the past ready to welcome you, the little girl crinkles her nose.

"It won't let you in," she says.

That's always been true before now. But somehow, you know beyond reason, it isn't true now. The first two times were a dress rehearsal. Now, this one is for keeps. This one is the end.

You drift toward the house, but the little girl tugs on your jacket.

"Don't go," she whispers. "It isn't safe in there."

You pull away from her. "It isn't safe out here either."

And with that, you head across the yard and onto the porch. The door creaks open before you, and without hesitating, you walk right in.

Inside, the house is exactly as you left it all those years ago. The ghost of beef stroganoff dinners seeped into the yellowed wallpaper. You're barely across the threshold when your eyes go heavy, your limbs weak, and as if on command, you hang up your jacket on the hallway coatrack, your cell phone still inside.

"Mom," you murmur, "I'm home."

The hallway extends before you, undulating like the sea, your feet unsteady beneath you. Your head whirls, but you try not to notice as you approach the last door on the left. It's your childhood bedroom, the Care Bears poster still taped to the wall, a mountain of stuffed animals moldering in a toybox.

And your mother is waiting for you inside, wearing a long black dress as if she's mourning something. As if she's mourning you.

"I knew you'd come," she says with a smile, and the walls tremble in reply. You realize all at once that everything in the house is damp for no reason, the floors soft as a sponge, the ceiling covered in moss and grit and something else, something viscous and writhing.

"Come here," your mother says, and like always, you do what you're told. Now that you're back in this house, it feels so natural to listen to your mother. To not even bother to argue.

You sit together on the daybed, the scent of rot rising all around you.

"Why have you done this?" you ask, your voice fading like a dream.

"Because I had to," your mother says, and you know that's the best answer you'll ever get. Because there's never any real reason. No explanation for why a mother would unravel the world or unravel her daughter.

She leans in closer, and you feel your body turn to jelly. Nothing about you feels like it belongs to you anymore. It feels like it belongs to her.

You swallow hard, and that's when you hear it. There's a strange vibration coming from the other room. It sounds like your cell phone, but it's so very far away now. Too far away to matter.

Despite yourself, you close your eyes, and your mother's arms tighten around you, so close you can barely breathe.

The house moans and contorts, the walls sealing around you like a cocoon. Soon, nobody will be able to get in. And nobody will be able to get out.

As the world starts to disintegrate around you, Mindy's voice is suddenly on repeat in your mind.

You don't need to stay there.

So long as you keep returning to your mother, this will never end. You'll be trapped in this loop until the end of time.

Of course, breaking this cycle shouldn't come down to you. It should never come down to the ones who already bear the weight of the world. Nobody ever should have asked you to come back. Nobody should have asked anything of you. You've surrendered too much already.

But even though you've spent years wishing it could be different, here's the one thing you never wanted to admit: you're the only one who can save yourself. Not this town, not even Mindy. Certainly not your mother.

When you were young, you didn't have a choice. This was your home, like it or not, and she was your mother, rage and thorns and all.

You get a choice now. Even as the walls close tighter around you, you still have a choice.

With the last wisps of strength wilting from your body, you wrench away from your mother and stumble toward the hallway. Her thin hands reach out for you, her arms lengthening, her skin gone slick and slimy, everything about her becoming longer, stranger, and more dangerous.

In the bedroom doorway, you glance back. Her face is shifting now, the same as the walls. Everything here is coming apart at the seams.

"You're mine," she says, her voice warbling, a distant melody of something from beyond echoing inside her.

"No," you say, "I'm not."

They're such simple words. So small they feel like nothing at all. But sometimes, it takes so little to break such a powerful spell. And that's what you've done. With three words, you've said goodbye.

On the way out, you grab your jacket and slip back inside your own life. Something calls out from the hall, but you pay it no mind. You just close the door behind you, not looking back.

Outside, the night air is warmer than you remember, and all the houses seem smaller than before. You don't know what will become of the town now. If it will crumble. If it'll just go on standing, the same way it always has.

But either way, it doesn't matter, not anymore, not to you. What matters is that you go home, your *real* home, the place you belong. Mindy is waiting there for you. She's always been waiting, hoping you come back to her.

As you start toward your car, your head tipped up, you see a family in a nearby driveway packing their lives into the trunk of their Subaru. Standing in the yard, a Hello Kitty bookbag on her back is the little girl in pigtails. With her gap-toothed grin, she waves brightly at you.

You nod and wave back. Then you keep walking.

You're almost downtown when your phone rings again. Mindy's voice is clear and eager on the other end.

"Selena?" she says, your name on her lips sounding like a sweet sermon.

"I'll be back by morning," you say. "I'll be back to stay."

A long moment. "Promise?" Mindy asks.

"I promise," you say.

As you climb into your car, the ground quivers beneath you, but you barely notice it now. The engine turns over, and you travel down Main Street for the last time, past the wreckage of a life you never asked for.

Up ahead, the skies are clear, the stars glimmering gold, and with the state highway unfurling before you, all you can do is smile as the vague mist of the past vanishes in the rearview mirror.

ABOUT SADIE HARTMANN

SADIE HARTMANN (aka Mother Horror) is the co-owner of the horror fiction subscription company Night Worms and the Bram Stoker Awards®-nominated editor of her own horror fiction imprint, Dark Hart. She is the author of 101 HORROR BOOKS TO READ BEFORE YOU'RE MURDERED.

She lives in the PNW with her husband of 20+ years, where they stare at Mt Rainier, eat street tacos, and hang out with their three kids. They have a Frenchie named Owen.

ABOUT THE EDITOR

Called a "champion for women's voices in horror" by *Shelf Awareness*, **LINDY RYAN** is the Bram Stoker Awards®-nominated and Silver Falchion Award-winning editor of INTO THE FOREST: TALES OF THE BABA YAGA. She has been named one of horror's most masterful anthology curators alongside Ellen Datlow and Christopher Golden, is the current author-in-residence at *Rue Morgue*, and was a 2020 *Publishers Weekly* Star Watch Honoree for her work at Black Spot Books, an independent press focused on amplifying underrepresented voices in horror. She is the author of BLESS YOUR HEART, COLD SNAP, and more, as well as an award-winning short film director for her children's picture book turned animated short, TRICK OR TREAT, ALISTAIR GRAY.

A long-time advocate for women-in-horror and an active member of the HWA, ITW, and the Brothers Grimm Society of North America, Ryan is the current co-chair of the HWA Publishers Council. The author of numerous works of fiction and nonfiction, Lindy's work has been adapted for film.

www.LindyRyanWrites.com

ABOUT THE AUTHORS

Jill Baguchinsky is the award-winning author of the young adult novels SO WITCHES WE BECAME, MAMMOTH, and SPOOKYGIRL. Fluent in darkness and Disney, Jill lives on the Gulf Coast of Florida, where she spends her summers dodging hurricanes and her winters wishing for cold fronts.

Carina Bissett is a writer and poet working primarily in the fields of dark fiction and fabulism. Her work has been published in numerous journals and anthologies including INTO THE FOREST: TALES OF THE BABA YAGA, UPON A TWICE TIME, BITTER DISTILLATIONS: AN ANTHOLOGY OF POISONOUS TALES, and ARTERIAL BLOOM. Her poetry has been nominated for the Pushcart Prize and the Sundress Publications Best of the Net and can be found in the HWA POETRY SHOWCASE, *Fantasy Magazine*, and *NonBinary Review*. She is also the co-editor of the award-winning anthology SHADOW ATLAS: DARK LANDSCAPES OF THE AMERICAS. Links to her work can be found at http://carinabissett.com.

Laura Cranehill lives in the Pacific Northwest with her spouse and three sons. Her work has appeared or is forthcoming in *Strange Horizons*, *Vastarien*, *[PANK]*, and elsewhere. She always eats up all the cookies her children bake.

Renee Cronley is a writer and nurse from Manitoba. She enjoys long walks in the cemetery and hates when people chew with their mouths open. Her work appears in *Chestnut Review*, *PRISM international*, *Off Topic*, *Love Letters to Poe*,

Weird Little Worlds, and several other anthologies and literary magazines.

L. E. Daniels is an awarded poet, editor, and author. Her novel SERPENT'S WAKE: A TALE FOR THE BITTEN is a Notable Work with the HWA's Mental Health Initiative. Lauren co-edited WE ARE PROVIDENCE, which appeared the Bram Stoker Awards® Preliminary Ballot and is a finalist for the 2022 Aurealis Award. She co-edited Aiki Flinthart's legacy anthology, RELICS, WRECKS AND RUINS (CAT Press) with Geneve Flynn, winning the 2021 Aurealis Award. For her poetry, she won the Newport Poetry Award in 1987 and her recent work appears in the HWA's OF HORROR AND HOPE, UNDER HER EYE (Black Spot Books), and DASTARDLY DAMSELS (Crystal Lake) anthologies. She's finalist for the 2022 Australian Shadows Award. An editor for over 100 titles, Lauren directs Brisbane Writers Workshop.

Kristi DeMeester is the author of SUCH A PRETTY SMILE, BENEATH, and the short fiction collection EVERYTHING THAT'S UNDERNEATH. Her short stories have appeared in BLACK STATIC and THE DARK, among others, and she's had stories included in several volumes of Ellen Datlow's THE BEST HORROR OF THE YEAR, YEAR'S BEST WEIRD FICTION, and Stephen Graham Jones's BEST NEW HORROR. She is at work on her next novel. Find her online at www.kristidemeester.com.

Carol Edwards is a northern California native transplanted to southern Arizona. She grew up reading fantasy and classic novels, climbing trees, and acquiring frequent grass stains. She currently enjoys a coffee addiction and raising her succulent army. Her poetry has been published in numerous anthologies, periodicals, and online blogs, including *Space & Time*, *Trouvaille Review*, *POETiCA REViEW*, *The Sunlight Press*, Red Penguin Books, Southern Arizona Press, White Stag Publishing, *The Post Grad Journal*, and Black Spot Books. Her debut poetry collection, THE WORLD EATS LOVE, released in April 2023 from The Ravens Quoth Press.

N.J. Ember is a paranormal fiction author who loves to write stories about survival and triumph over adversity. Whether her characters are dealing with the paranormal or everyday life, she seeks to show that strength is not always about being superhuman or invulnerable. She currently lives in Michigan with her grandpa, her partner, and their dog.

Bram Stoker Awards®-nominated **Meg Hafdahl** is the creator of numerous stories and books. Her fiction has appeared in anthologies such as EVE'S REQUIEM: TALES OF WOMEN, MYSTERY and HORROR AND ECLECTICALLY CRIMINAL. Her work has been produced for audio by *The Wicked Library* and *The Lift*, and she is the author of three popular short story collections including TWISTED REVERIES: THIRTEEN TALES OF THE MACABRE. Meg is also the author of the three novels: THE DARKEST HUNGER, DAUGHTERS OF DARKNESS, and HER DARK INHERITANCE. She is the co-host of the podcast Horror Rewind and co-author of THE SCIENCE OF MONSTERS, THE SCIENCE OF WOMEN IN HORROR, THE SCIENCE OF STEPHEN KING, THE SCIENCE OF SERIAL KILLERS, THE SCIENCE OF WITCHCRAFT, THE SCIENCE OF AGATHA CHRISTIE, and the upcoming TRAVELS OF TERROR. She lives in the snowy bluffs of Minnesota with her husband, sons, and a menagerie of pets.

M. Halstead is an all-the-time graphic designer and sometimes author. She dabbles in drabbles, short fiction, and comics, and also enjoys traditional printmaking and zinemaking. Her areas of interest include dark fiction and horror, especially through the lens of queerness and transgressive art. She currently resides in North Carolina with her husband and two cats. Although she eschews most social media, you can find her online at mhalstead.com.

Rachel Harrison is the national bestselling author of BLACK SHEEP, CACKLE, SUCH SHARP TEETH, and THE RETURN, which was nominated for a Bram Stoker Award for Superior Achievement in a First Novel. Her short fiction has appeared in *Guernica*, *Electric Literature*'s Recommended Reading, as an Audible Original, and in her debut story collection BAD DOLLS. She lives in Western New York with her husband and their cat/overlord.

Emily Holi is an author, speculative fiction/satire writer, mom of five, and grilled cheese connoisseur. She currently balances writing (at her kitchen counter) with constant-laundry-folding, magnatile-tower-constructing, and round-the-clock-sandwich-making.

Gwendolyn Kiste is the Bram Stoker® and Lambda Literary Award-winning author of THE RUST MAIDENS, RELUCTANT IMMORTALS, PRETTY MARYS ALL IN A ROW, and THE HAUNTING OF VELKWOOD. She resides on an abandoned horse farm with her husband, their calico cat, and not nearly enough ghosts. Find her at gwendolynkiste.com.

Lisa Kröger is a horror writer, podcaster, and short film producer. Her book MONSTER, SHE WROTE won the Bram Stoker Award® for Superior Achievement in Nonfiction and the Locus Award for Best Nonfiction. Following the success of MONSTER, SHE WROTE, Valancourt Books launched a *Monster, She Wrote* book series, which now includes five titles. Lisa is a co-host of the Know Fear Cast and Monster, She Wrote podcasts. With Nyx Horror Collective, she produced *13 Minutes of Horror*, a short film festival for women filmmakers, which streamed on Shudder in 2021 and 2022. Her newest book is TOIL AND TROUBLE: A WOMEN'S HISTORY OF THE OCCULT.

Brooke MacKenzie is the author of the short fiction collection GHOST GAMES, which Kirkus Reviews called, "[a]n indelible batch of nightmarish tales," and the horror poetry collection, THE SCARY ABECEDARY. Her short fiction, poetry, and essays have been published in numerous magazines and anthologies, and she has had two of her stories produced as podcast episodes by The Nights End Podcast. She lives in a delightfully haunted town in Northern California with her husband and daughter. For more about Brooke, visit her website: www.bamackenzie.com, or find her on Instagram: @mackbrookpro.

Caitlin Marceau is a queer author and illustrator based in Montreal. She holds a Bachelor of Arts in Creative Writing, is an Active Member of the Horror Writers Association, and has spoken about genre literature at several Canadian conventions. Her work includes FEMINA, A BLACKNESS ABSOLUTE, and THIS IS WHERE WE TALK THINGS

OUT. Her second novella, I'M HAVING REGRETS, and her debut novel, IT WASN'T SUPPOSED TO GO LIKE THIS, are set for publication in 2024. For more, visit CaitlinMarceau.ca or find her on social media.

Jessica McHugh is a two-time Bram Stoker Awards®-nominated poet, a multi-genre novelist, and an internationally produced playwright who spends her days surrounded by artistic inspiration at a Maryland tattoo shop. She's had thirty books published in fifteen years, including her Elgin Award-nominated blackout poetry collection, A COMPLEX ACCIDENT OF LIFE her sci-fi bizarro romp, THE GREEN KANGAROOS, and her cross-generational horror series, *The Gardening Guidebooks Trilogy*. Explore the growing worlds of Jessica McHugh at McHughniverse.com.

Emma E. Murray's stories have appeared in anthologies like *What One Wouldn't Do*, *Obsolescence*, and *Ooze: Little Bursts of Body Horror* as well as magazines such as *CHM* and *Pyre*. Her chapbook, *Exquisite Hunger*, is available from Medusa Haus, and her novella, *When the Devil*, as well as her debut novel, *Crushing Snails*, will be coming out in 2024. To read more, you can visit her website EmmaEMurray.com

Lee Murray is a multi-award-winning writer and poet, and a five-time Bram Stoker Awards® winner, including for poetry for TORTURED WILLOWS (with Christina Sng, Angela Yuriko Smith, and Geneve Flynn). A NZSA Honorary Literary Fellow, Lee is a Grimshaw Sargeson Fellow and winner of the NZSA Laura Solomon Cuba Press Prize for her forthcoming prose-poetry collection FOX SPIRIT ON A DISTANT CLOUD. She is an Elgin Award runner up, and a Rhysling-,

Dwarf Star-, and Pushcart-nominated poet. Her poem ‹cheongsam› won the Australian Shadows Award for poetry for 2021. Her poetry anthology UNDER HER EYE (co-edited with Lindy Ryan), a women-in-horror project in association with the Pixels Project to prevent violence against women, releases in Nov 2023 from Black Spot Books. Read more at leemurray.info

Christi Nogle is the author of the Shirley Jackson Award nominated and Bram Stoker Awards®-winning First Novel BEULAH from Cemetery Gates Media as well as the collections THE BEST OF OUR PAST, THE WORST OF OUR FUTURE and PROMISE from Flame Tree Press. She is co-editor with Willow Dawn Becker of the Bram Stoker Awards®-nominated anthology MOTHER: TALES OF LOVE AND TERROR and co-editor with Ai Jiang of WILTED PAGES: AN ANTHOLOGY OF DARK ACADEMIA. Follow her at http://christinogle.com and on Twitter @christinogle.

Tanya Pell is a horror and dark fantasy writer living near Charlotte, NC with her family and rescue dogs. Her short horror fiction can be found in OBSOLESCENCE, *Shortwave Magazine*, and *Well, This is Tense.* Her novels are represented by Cortney Radocaj of Belcastro Agency. You can find her at tanyapell.com or on Twitter at @tanyacarinae.

A Tampa Bay native, **Crystal Sidell** grew up playing with toads in the rain and indulging in speculative fiction. She is a Pushcart Nominee and Rhsyling Finalist, with poems appearing in *Apparition Lit, F&SF, Frozen Wavelets, Under Her Eye,* and others. Find her online at https://crystalsidell.wixsite.com/mysite.

Teagan Olivia Sturmer is a librarian and children's and adult author living on the stormy shores of Lake Superior, passionate about writing stories of girls who are stronger than they know. Teagan graduated from Northern Michigan University with a degree in Creative Writing and used that to pursue her love of Shakespeare, acting and directing in her local theatre, and studying the art of dramaturgy. Having been diagnosed with General Anxiety Disorder and PTSD for most of her life, Teagan is passionate about telling stories of resilience. Short stories of Teagan's can be found in anthologies from Phantom House Press, Quill and Crow Publishing, Shortwave Publishing, and Eerie River Publishing. Teagan lives in Michigan's wild Upper Peninsula with her husband, their pups, and one rather persnickety calico cat. She is represented by Amy Giuffrida of the Belcastro Agency.

Roxie Voorhees is a tangled threesome of Gag me with a Spoon, Welcome to the Darkside, and Catch me Outside. They are author of THE LONGEST THIRST, a splatterwestern, and co-editor of MINE and READER BEWARE.

Jacqueline West is a novelist and poet living in Minnesota. Her work has appeared in the recent anthologies CHROMOPHOBIA and INTO THE FOREST, as well as in *Tales from the Moonlit Path*, *Strange Horizons*, *Mirror Dance*, and *Liminality*. Her books for young readers include the NYT-bestselling dark fantasy series *The Books of Elsewhere*, the YA horror novel LAST THINGS, and the award-winning ghost story "Long Lost." Find her online at jacquelinewest.com.

Stephanie M. Wytovich is an American poet, novelist, and essayist. Her work has been showcased in numerous magazines and anthologies such as *Weird Tales*, *Nightmare Magazine*, *Southwest Review*, YEAR'S BEST HARDCORE HORROR: VOLUME 2, THE BEST HORROR OF THE YEAR: VOLUME 8 & 15, as well as many others. Wytovich is the Poetry Editor for Raw Dog Screaming Press, and an adjunct at Western Connecticut State University, Southern New Hampshire University, and Point Park University. Her Bram Stoker Awards®-winning poetry collection, BROTHEL, earned a home with Raw Dog Screaming Press alongside HYSTERIA: A COLLECTION OF MADNESS, MOURNING JEWELRY, AN EXORCISM OF ANGELS, SHEET MUSIC TO MY ACOUSTIC NIGHTMARE, and THE APOCALYPTIC MANNEQUIN. Her debut novel, THE EIGHTH, is published with Dark Regions Press, and her nonfiction craft book for speculative poetry, WRITING POETRY IN THE DARK, is available now from Raw Dog Screaming Press. Follow on Twitter and Instagram @SWytovich and @thehauntedbookshelf.

Kelsea Yu is the Shirley Jackson Award-nominated author of BOUND FEET and IT'S ONLY A GAME. She has over a dozen short stories and essays forthcoming or published in various magazines and anthologies including *Clarkesworld*, *PseudoPod*, *Fantasy*, and more. Find her on Instagram as @anovelescape or visit her website kelseayu.com.

OTHER ANTHOLOGIES FROM BLACK SPOT BOOKS

Classic Monsters Unleashed, *Edited by James Aquilone*
Into the Forest: Tales of the Baba Yaga, *Edited by Lindy Ryan*
Unquiet Spirits: Essays by Asian Women in Horror,
Edited by Lee Murray and Angela Yuriko Smith